SKYLINE

THE DRAGON COMMANDER

KENNEDY KING

MIND OF KHAN STUDIOS

Written by Kennedy King

Edited by HG Productions

Cover Art by HG Productions

GET A FREE FICTION ADVENTURE FROM ME

When the Monsters Come: A Science Fiction Horror Experience (Shadows Beyond the Stars Book 1)

When the Standing Ones sent us on a journey to explore the darkness far from the sun's light, I never expected to find monsters there.

Like something out of the scary tales my son so loved, they captured us while I slumbered.

I woke with my crew, locked away in a cold thundercloud colored cage.

The others looked to me for escape but all my plans had ended in failure and pain, so much pain.

At the same time, the monsters began to take them away one by one.

Pushing past those failures and the pain, I plotted my escape, I was born problem solver after all.

I needed to warn my people of what awaited us among the stars and to see my boy again.

To do so, I'd have to discover more about these monsters and their ways, revolting as that seemed.

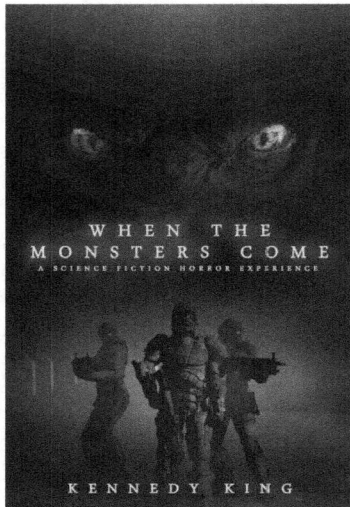

Get your free copy by joining my mailing list at,

https://kennedykingauthor.com/join-my-newsletter/

CONTENTS

Acknowledgement

Thank you to my family, my friends and my wonderful readers who have been enjoying this adventure with me as I write and release a journey at a time.
Get your fill of even more fiction goodness at my official website, www.kennedykingauthor.com and sign up for my official email list as well for more treats, https://kennedykingauthor.com/join-my-newsletter/

1

COLLIDING WORLDS

THE FIRST TIME Finch's shimmering station pass beeped in rejection, he attributed it to the Precinct he'd been assigned. Everyone in Shanghai and the surrounding metroscape knew what kind of shape Precinct 117 was in. The recent influx of those crazy nanotech sentries from the WCC helped, and there weren't many fringe extremists against them this side of China, but Finch was getting ahead of himself. He needed to get inside first. He swiped the card three more times before he thought it might be another test. Between his new partner and his rumpled old supervisor, the tests had hardly ended with his graduation from the academy. The door beeped back the red shut-out light every time.

"Just my luck..." Finch muttered, seemingly to himself. The wall-mounted speaker crackled alive.

"If you're going to fall back on *luck,* you might as well leave your badge on the step, rookie," grumbled the doorman. So he *was* listening.

"Door lock still busted? Or is it my card?" said Finch.

"Probably both," laughed the doorman. The door swung out with a push from another rookie from his office. It was the young man only a few years Finch's senior, who held the desk directly across from his. Of all the people Finch had met in his three weeks on the force, Greg was the only one he could form a remote connection to.

"We've got bots that can be a table or a gun, but no functioning door," Greg shook his head while he let Finch in. He sucked down a deep breath of cool, pure air. Finch was still adjusting to the transition from the overcrowded, humid haze of Shanghai's regular atmosphere to the filtered inside of a WCC-supported Precinct.

"So why didn't you send your Squire to let me in?" Finch raised a sandy blonde eyebrow.

"New ordinance. Costs the Precinct millions more to pay for the Squires than it does for us. They don't lift a shapeshifting finger unless it's something we *can't* do ourselves," said Greg.

They headed through the glum halls to their office. The shimmering teal track of tube lights overhead made everything visible, but in such a drab light it made the Precinct even more depressing than it was by default. Sure, some Precincts in India and Afghanistan saw action, but 117 was a relic of times before the WCC, before the SkyLine changed everything. A time when law needed enforcing, when the life of the planet wasn't at stake.

"While we're on Squires... how are things with your new partner?" asked Greg, while they paced. Finch took a glance down every crossing hallway before he started.

"Strange. Really strange. I mean - I knew it'd be weird, with his... what's-it-called, a personality matrix?" fumbled Finch.

"Yeah. I could hardly believe it when I heard. A drone with a heart of gold," said Greg.

"Don't know about gold... but he does apologize for *everything*. And he's a little... clingy? Always asking me if I'm alright, or if I need anything. Wouldn't be surprised if it was *him* driving the Precinct bills through the roof," Finch marveled. That was around the time Finch and Greg made it to their office. A grid of cubicles adorned with glowing instant-coffee canisters and splayed manila files made it more their homes than their tiny, stacked one-room apartments.

"Well, the software *is* in beta. Poor guy is just a kink to be worked out," said Greg. He sunk into his worn, swivel office chair. "Didn't they give him a human-sounding model number too? No wonder the thing's confused." Greg spun in his chair to face his desk just before a digitized voice piped up behind Finch's head.

"Mr. Finch!"

"Ah! DA-Vos, too loud!" Finch gasped. He wheeled to face a black onyx oval, the faceless face of his partner. Finch could see the whites of his own eyes in the reflective surface inches away. "And too close."

"Sorry, Mr. Finch! I am still adjusting my proximity settings for appropriate socialization," said DA-Vos. The jet-black, seamless, man-shaped machine took one small step back.

"How about one more step? Let's say... two feet between us, at all times?" said Finch.

"Yes, very good, Mr. Finch," said DA-Vos, the glossy black of his face lighting lavender when he spoke. Purely for human convenience, the chief had explained, Squires with a personality matrix were assigned a gender. According to this odd rule, DA-Vos was officially a "he". First it made Finch laugh, when it was so common for *people* to change genders as they grew into themselves. Then the less humorous idea of rights for thinking machines poked into his mind.

"And drop the Mr. too. Just Finch is fine," he forced himself not to mumble *for the fifth time.*

"Yes, of course, Mr. Finch," said DA-Vos. Finch groaned. Greg's chuckles, while his own Squire sat silently beside him, didn't help. Finch almost jumped back when DA-Vos jerked up his arm. His shapeless, metallic tentacle reformed itself before Finch's eyes into a perfect imitation of a human hand. He sighed, and took DA-Vos' glossy new fingers for a firm shake.

"DA-Vos, I... appreciate the gesture, but handshakes are typically at the beginning or end of a conversation. And maybe a little less abrupt? You're going to scare someone if you do that outside the Precinct," Finch told him. A long breath escaped him when he remembered he hadn't even clocked in yet. Finch's brother was off in a lab somewhere developing faster Fusion jets for magnetrains, and here *he* was parenting a gigantic, robotic man-baby in the slums. *Just my luck,* he thought, and this time he meant it.

"Understood, Mr. Finch... apologies, but my analytics show that after three weeks as partners, we should be more closely bonded. I was only extending a friendly gesture," said DA-Vos. Then the light on his face glowed blue. Sure there was an AI in there, running the whole nanotech show.

Sure, Finch knew some immeasurably complex code was calculating the closest thing a computer could simulate to "emotion". Still, he couldn't have been prepared for the words that came through that blue glow. "Why do you not like me, Mr. Finch?" Finch could only stare into the radiating metal, in search of the mind inside.

"DA-Vos... it's not that I don't like you," said Finch. How best to say this, to so new a psyche, natural, or artificial? "Humans don't run on analytics. And... you can't force a bond. It just has to happen. It's part of being partners."

"I see..." DA-Vos' face glow returned to its neutral lavender. Then the door from the main entrance slammed shut, marking the Chief's entrance. Every officer, human and Squire, straightened up before his procession.

"At ease, you beanbags," the Chief grumbled. "Office meeting in five. Time for your new route assignments." On his way, he took a deep glowing pull from his cigarano. The health benefits of vaporized sage and chamomile filled the Chief's chest with each deep breath. He disappeared behind the door to his office with no further word. The office resumed its previous casual shuffle.

"Think his blood vessels would burst if we hid that thing from him?" whispered Greg, about the cigarano. Finch turned to answer, but stopped when he noticed a color he'd never seen before, on DA-Vos' face. His light smoldered yellow.

"DA-Vos?"

"Do... do you not hear that?" murmured DA-Vos.

"Hear what?" said Finch. Greg turned full around to face both man and Squire.

"Do... do robots understand humor? Is that a joke?" said Greg.

"No... no joke... it's..." DA-Vos's yellow tint deepened, brightened, to show his concentration on something unheard to the others. "Do what? You want me to... no. I said *no!*"

Greg's hand flew for his pistol too late. The sharpened spearhead arm of his own partner pierced him through. The Squire pinned his gushing back to his desk. When Greg slumped away, it turned its light, now crimson metal face on Finch, too shaken to move. It's arm reconfigured into an open-ended barrel, swimming with prismatic light. DA-Vos' body opened as a black steel blanket around his partner just in time. The Squire fired three shining lasers before it moved on to another officer, at another desk.

"Remain quiet, and still, Mr. Finch," said DA-Vos' voice, inside the black dome of his reformed mass. His purple face-light glowed in the dark.

"A-alright..." Finch whimpered. His partner's body kept him safe from the Fusion rays, but only muffled the screams. He could still hear every last one of his fellow officers blown away, skewered, and incinerated by their Squire partners.

In the lavender dark, Finch felt every word about the bond between partners like a knot in his stomach. He felt rather differently about his luck, too.

-

Major General Christopher Droan. It sounded so impressive. It sounded so profound. Just what his dad would have wanted for him. What it *didn't* sound like was just what it was: a magnetrain ride from the literal and figurative forest of high-rise towers in Beijing to a pointlessly huge office. It wasn't always this way. There were times, before man-machine partnerships had become standard, before the WCC supplied their Precincts with Fusion equipment, when Major General meant what it sounded like. Missions. Fire-fights. Eradication of the last few fringe groups still that opposed the World Crisis Council. Still, Chris left his desk full of cases to manage, with a certain skip in his step. He hung by a muscular arm from the overhead rail of the speeding magnetrain with a grin on his face. He would trade it all again, for what he had now. The Precincts and their Squires could have the sprawling cityscapes of layered apartments, offices, and vertical garden terraces. He had his apartment on the sixteenth floor, where he raced to now, and his apartment had the only thing he really needed.

"Sheba!" Chris popped the lock on their apartment door with his key card. "Did you get my message? I'm so sorry I'm late!"

"Late?" Sheba cut him short. He followed her voice with a chuckle, to their kitchen. "This show doesn't play without the both of us. You're never late."

"I'd consider myself lucky to be your stagehand," Chris laughed. Then he turned the corner, saw her, and the words ran right out of his head. Her dark, smooth skin shone a mixture of silver from the Fusion tube lighting overhead and orange from the candle on the table. When she stood, dark curls spun around the, rich golden-brown rings in her eyes. She gave Chris a spin of her fierce ruby dress. The fabric swept up to flash her full thighs. She opened her arms to the chair pulled out for him.

"Oh Sheba, you didn't have to..." Chris struggled to find anything he could say to feel he deserved this.

"Of course I did! We never had our proper engagement dinner!" said Sheba, "Now sit. I'm sure you're starving, and I'm itching to get out of this dress." Another wink was all it took to pin Chris to his seat. He wasn't even sure what it was she'd made, with how quickly he inhaled it. It was delicious, though.

Around him and Sheba was a vortex of colliding worlds. This was a newer apartment complex, wired with Fusion tubing for all the modern commodities a young couple could want, in 2350. After relocating to an office to get an apartment away from the barracks, though, Chris and Sheba could only just afford furniture and decorations. The two found themselves unexpectedly grateful for the storage locker of collectibles Chris' father had left them. His love for antiques had passed to his son but created a jarring visual as decor in their apartment. Silver food storage units defrosted and froze food in seconds, beside an old clock that still *ticked.* An oven could cook a piece of meat through in four blinks while a deep-cushioned rocking chair creaked in the living room. Anything beat the barracks, though. Over these past months, Chris and Sheba had even come to love it - differences had never been an obstacle for them.

"I hope you aren't too tired," said Chris, when at last he wiped the corner of his mouth.

"Not if *you're* willing to do most of the work, after your long day," said Sheba, red-lipped smile glistening. He'd been excited since he walked in, enthralled since he saw that dress; Chris couldn't wait another second. Sheba leaned back in her chair, feigning the helpless damsel. "Oh, Major General, *please* whisk me away," she moaned. Chris hoisted her up in both arms and carried her to their bedroom.

"Consider yourself whisked," he whispered. He caught a glimpse of himself in the glass panes of a window on the way. His hazel eyes jumped out from the sharp lines of his face. His tufts of auburn hair swayed across his tan skin, already glinting with a certain thrill. The briefest thought crossed his mind: *what did I do to deserve this?* He followed the teal glass tubes of Fusion lights down the hall and laid his fiancée on their bed, beside another candle. He flipped the lights.

Chris crawled over her and slipped his smile between hers. Warmth bound them together, then wetness. Their lips locked, loosened, and grazed. Sheba's legs slid apart so Chris could take a knee between them, like he'd taken a knee for her in their favorite park. He worked his mouth down her neck, feeling the pores prickle alive. He kissed the ridge of her breast, her stomach, all the way down to those dark thighs. With her heat still on his face, he slipped the skirt of her dress up. The arch of Sheba's shoulders to help get it off told him she was ready. She snapped up and seized his clothes into two claws of long nails. She tore them off and tossed them away with deft grace. Sheba's arms locked around his neck and pulled him down. She reached for the pulsing muscle between his legs, and put it against her. Chris pushed gently inside.

Chris and Sheba let out a deep breath together. The next minutes, hours, bled together in a churning sea of emotion and physical sensation. Tense muscles. Warm skin. Lips. The graze of fingers across nipples. Sheba crossed her legs behind Chris' hips to take him in as deep as she could. She arched her back again and clasped her fingers with his. Their love yanked the bed from the wall before Chris gave five last deep rocks and the two shared moments of climax, seconds apart. Bursts of colors played behind the closed eyes of concentration while they gasped and throbbed and groaned. Almost immediately, Chris collapsed beside his fiancée.

"Amazing..." mumbled Sheba, legs still trembling with aftershocks of pleasure.

"I know... and I don't even have to try," Chris joked, to a slap on the arm. He rolled over on his side, to gaze into big brown eyes. He and Sheba worked together to unwrinkle the sheets over them both.

"Are you... excited?" asked Sheba, to break the amorous silence.

"Not quite so much as I was minutes ago," said Chris. Sheba's eyes went wide with disbelief, but he had to get it out *somewhere.* The others at Chris' office were hardly the humorous type, at least around the Major General.

"About the wedding, Chris!" said Sheba, which of course, he knew.

"You mean the wedding *planning.* And as a matter of fact, I am," Chris assured her. He sat half up when he realized his mistake. "Not that that means we have to figure it all out tonight." Sheba laughed at the honest panic in his voice. He knew they could, too, if he gave Sheba the reins. Two of her favorite things: planning *and* a wedding, especially her own? But Chris wanted to be part of it, too.

"How about a location?" Sheba prompted. Her eagerness was irresistible.

"How... specific do we need to get?" said Chris.

"Let's start with which planet," said Sheba. Though he'd grown in a life with two worlds, Chris had never left Earth, and so the notion was still a culture shock for him. When he and Sheba were dating, and she first told him she hailed from the big red marble, rather than the blue one, he couldn't believe it. She seemed so human - more than that; charming, provocative. Before he met her, Chris had believed his father's old prejudice that people born in Mars' colonies would be more... alien.

"What do you think?" said Chris, "No matter where we plan it, one of our families will have to cross the SkyLine to get there."

"Maybe we should have it somewhere out there, then?" said Sheba. Chris snorted.

"On the SkyLine? Please, I don't need to seem any more like an Earthlocked tourist than I already do," Chris waved it off. Sheba's eyes glossed over.

"Then... you'd go to Mars? You'd drag your whole family out there?" said Sheba.

"If you were set on having the wedding there." Chris knew it was so much easier said than done. His father's prejudice against Cold Fusion technology, the resultant AI-driven robots, and just about everything else that came from the mines on the red planet, ran deep in their veins.

"Chris... I love you. I don't know if I can ever tell you how much," said Sheba, "Which is why we'll do it on Earth. Your family might be more... receptive on their own turf."

"I love you, too," smiled Chris. They leaned for a kiss just before the shrill ring of their ancient phone rattled its hook. Chris had to have a special port installed for the land-line they inherited from his dad, since affording Fusion phones was entirely out of the question for them now. Chris would have let it ring itself out, but for the fact that there were only two other places connected to their house on the archaic line. It was either his job, or a job offer for Sheba. "Hello?" he sighed into the receiver.

"Who is it?" murmured Sheba, while Chris' face darkened.

"WCC," he whispered, still listening. Each word seemed to yank his heartstrings tighter. "I... are you sure? Yes, I know you wouldn't call if you weren't... yes... I understand..." Chris reached for his pants.

"Good Lord, what is it, Chris?"

"I'll be there as soon as I can," Chris said, before clicking the phone back down. His eyes fell heavy on Sheba. "I have to go to the WCC consulate... there's been an attack."

2

DARK DEVELOPMENTS

"AN ATTACK?" Sheba blurted, almost laughing at the absurdity. It was almost ten o'clock, and they called to tell Chris about an *attack*? "I'm sure there has been. In the mountains, in the fields. Far, far away from Beijing, I'm sure there's been plenty of attacks. Isn't that what the WCC supplies Precincts for? Chris... what?" Sheba shifted upright when she saw true distress sink into the lines on his face. She'd seen them rarely, even when they lived at the barracks. As it always had, the look preceded Chris unlocking the case under the bed, to retrieve his dad's old pistol.

"The attack was *on* one of the Precincts. 117, in Shanghai," said Chris. Unprecedented as something like that was, since the widespread distribution of Squires, Sheba breathed herself into a calm.

"That *is* peculiar... but aren't there other Precincts nearby that can help? What makes it a WCC concern?" she tried, tears welling in her eyes. The pistol in his belt was never a good sign.

"The Squires the WCC sent there turned on their partners," Chris told her.

"My God... Chris..." Sheba mumbled. She hugged the sheets up around her while Chris shouldered his jacket and holstered his pistol, a six-chamber revolver as polished as the day his dad had given it. He faced her, as disappointed as she was, but the sudden shift of her expression disarmed Chris. It wasn't just disappointment. It wasn't just anger. Sheba looked terrified. "Please don't go."

"Sheba..." Chris whispered, swooping to the edge of the bed beside her. Never once in their five years together had she demanded that of him. "What is it?" Her eyes went wide again at the question. "Sheba..." She ran through every reasonable response in her mind, anything but the truth. She didn't need to worry him more.

"It's... I've just been having trouble sleeping. Been thinking about the wedding and all... I really need you here," pleaded Sheba. Tears poked up in the corners of her eyes. Chris' hand flung to brush them away, but she turned her head to do it herself.

"Sheba, I'm sorry... I need to be here, too. I'm so sorry I can't be, just tonight. This is that rare time when I *have* to answer," Chris reassured her.

"I know, I know... I'm sorry," Sheba turned back to him, smiling. She'd known from the moment the phone hung up that he was going. Not even she could stop him, and she'd opened a dangerous door. Sheba *had* been having trouble sleeping of late, but it had nothing to do with the wedding. "You have to go, I understand."

"I wish you didn't have to... Sheba, is that really all? I've never seen you like this, not over work," Chris raised an eyebrow of true, wounding concern.

"That's really all, Chris. I promise. Now you go. It'd be selfish for me to keep you here for myself, when you've got a job to do," she smiled her way into another long, wet kiss. "Go keep us all safe. I love you."

"I love you too," Chris replied, like he wasn't just as concerned. He lingered by the door to their bedroom when it closed behind him. He waited to hear anything, any small hint to what could *really* be plaguing Sheba so deeply she would keep it from even him. All he heard were sobs. When Chris wanted nothing more than to go back through their bedroom door, he zipped his jacket and headed outside.

-

Sheba wanted so badly to keep it together, for Chris. She *had* to, she told herself. That minor breach was almost too much. If there really *had* been a malfunction so profound in the AIs, he had enough on his plate. He didn't have to know about her dreams. Not yet. It wasn't like she was full-blown 3D... not yet.

Still, when she lay in the dark, eyes too wide for tears, she remembered how her uncle had started the same way. Dreams. He dismissed it, like most did, that worked the mines on the red planet where she grew. Cases of dragon dissociation disorder have plummeted since the shallow mine movement in 3200, after all. But there was always a reason for a movement like that. In this case, it was the sheer number of Martian miners succumbing to delusion.

The elements under Mars' crust were the heart of Cold Fusion technology, the heart of human survival, but so too the cause of rampant hallucinations.

Even after hours in the mines, an unidentified whisper or flash of light could manifest. After days, miners heard voices speak in tongues they could not. Weeks of prolonged exposure meant nightmares, like the ones Sheba was having now. Months without a vacation from the Martian Fusion Mines could be downright paralytic. People were tormented, asleep or awake. What caused such radical change in practice, and earned the condition the monicker 3D, was the nature of the delusions. Every miner, and even some technicians, were haunted by the same image. Fearsome beasts glowering in the dark. Scales in place of skin. Yellow glow behind glassy lenses, with a flash of claws instead of hands or feet. They looked closest to what old Earthlocked legends called Dragons. Giving them a name, though, was little consolation for the people who heard and saw them nonstop. For decades, Mars saw a massive spread of asylums and a migration of psychologists to treat the sufferers of dragon dissociation disorders. Sheba figured she must be the only one who made the pilgrimage in reverse, but she just *had* to get away from all of that.

Sheba never worked the mines, but her uncle did. He was a lifetime resident at Red Star Asylum now, but once, he'd lived with her and her dad. She shuddered at the possible connection between that, and her dreams. She never once thought the end of his road might be hers too, but then she never thought spending time around the residue from the mines could give her nightmares all these years later. Perhaps it was even genetic? Just last night, Sheba saw the yellow eyes in the dark of sleep. She woke up with the whispers still in her ears. She thought about telling Chris more than once, but the excitement of their engagement was still so new. Sheba would never forgive herself if she quenched the fire of that with ungrounded worry.

They were just dreams, she told herself, alone in the dark. Still, Sheba lay awake, long after Chris went. She stared into the ceiling, trying to chase out the image of yellow gemstone eyes. Sheba let out a shaky breath. Just dreams.

-

"Ow! Rookie mistake, Tim," he whispered to himself, shaking out the finger he'd just nicked. It was all the company he had to talk to- well, himself, and his patients. By the time he was done with what he always thought was important work, those patients might just be able to answer him. For now, Tim just counted himself lucky to have found a company willing to invest in him. Months ago, Tim Carver had been another shut-in with a workshop in his mom's basement. Now, he was a shut-in with a *garage* workshop and a startup contract, in his own apartment on the wrong side of Beijing. "We can both do better, can't we?" he whispered to his current patient.

Tim fell back from the lamplight on a patiently sitting robot, and flicked on another to find the bandages. He wrapped his bleeding finger, which immediately stained the cloth. Tim sighed into a laugh. He was more intimately familiar with the insides of a Fusion Operation System than some men twice his age, and his scarred hands showed it. FOS design, for the most part, took more strength of will and mind than muscle, but some pain tolerance was necessary. Especially when fatigue set in. Tim hadn't fumbled a tool so hard in years. But that was how important this project was, to him at least. Tim might not have been in the part of town he wanted, or the country, or planet, but at least he had these projects. Nanoverse had given him a path to purpose, he reminded himself.

He'd been working on this particular home-service model for two weeks. It wasn't so different from WCC's Squires, but shrunken to the size of a child. Tim had been tasked with teaching the model something its human counterpart could never hope to: how to develop its own intelligence beyond the scope of its FOS, its AI, its brain. Thus far, the problem-solving software had melted down sixteen times, in sixteen tests. Tim had spent the better part of four days with his long spine arched over a screen, twisting and stretching various elements of the model's AI. Now it was time to test it. He just needed to create the problem, which is where the scalpel he cut himself on came in. One more careful swipe carved a sufficient slice. Tim took a step back from the robot, and said,

"TE-Les, on." The onyx child's face lit with a red beam of awareness. A single infrared beam swept across TE-Les' ocular slit, taking in the room and its master. Tim preferred the term *doctor*. He had to believe a deeper, more complex relationship was possible between them than designer and object, servant and master. It was the whole premise of his work at Nanoverse.

"Hello, Tim," said the robotic voice of a child. He'd designed the vocal range of this particular in-home-service model himself. The default deep, mature voice was too jarring from so small a body.

"How do you feel tonight, TE-Les?" posed Tim.

"Positively splendid," said TE-Les. Tim raised an eyebrow.

"Even though you know what I'm going to ask you to do? Even though it hasn't worked so well before?" Tim prodded. TE-Les gave a laser-flashing nod. At least the gesture training was working.

"Yes. I can feel that something is... different. It may not work this time, but perhaps the results will be interesting," said TE-Les, in a voice that almost sounded like a faceless smile.. *Interesting.* Tim had muttered just that to himself at the end of countless hours at this very workbench. TE-Les must have picked it up from him..

"You feel it, huh? I think you could be right," said Tim, knowing that emotional matrices were still in beta, and not in any Nanoverse models. He poked his bandaged finger at the slice he'd carved himself in the model's chest. "TE-Les, you've been damaged. Repair yourself," Tim said. Even after the first sixteen attempts, he still winced at this part. In previous trials, he had seen every reaction from mortified screams to sparks, smoke, and rampant form-changing. This time, TE-Les' visual laser swept over Tim's wounded hand, then her own chest. In his pipedream hope the TE-Les project would move on to some personality matrix work - he had customized the model as a "she".

"I cannot. My nanotech self-repair protocol's have been disabled," TE-Les realized, puzzled. Tim couldn't help himself. He let an exhausted cackle through his laced fingers. Never once had she made it past realizing her systems were tampered with. She'd never been able to say it.

"That's right, they have... what can we do about that, TE-Les?" prompted Tim. Her head tilted up. Her red laser swept him again. She didn't have the expression lights the WCC's Squires did, or the software to *feel,* let alone express it, which made it all the more chilling when she said,

"Why did you do this to me, Tim?" It was the sort of thing that made even an experienced FOS designer take a big step back, the old myth of the ghost in the machine.

"Wha-what?"

"Your blood pressure and perspiration suggest a mix of emotions. It does not seem you *wanted* to cause me damage, yet you did. Why?"

"TE-Les, you're veering outside the deviation accounted for by our tests," Tim shivered. Then it hit him, twice as hard as his own hand that slapped his forehead. "That's the whole point, isn't it? You're doing it. Trying to learn what your systems aren't equipped to accept... alright, TE-Les," sighed Tim, trying to muster up a way to say it, "My job is to make you make your*self* better. If you can learn to learn, unsupervised, there won't be a problem too complex for you to handle. You'll be able to help people... who can't tell you what they need. Nonverbal people... people who are hurt. Do you understand?"

"Yes," said TE-Les, "You damaged me to improve me." Her laser flashed across Tim's watery eyes, while he swept them dry. "If you altered my capabilities, could you not change them back?" He could only smile and nod at the ingenuity. Tim wasn't sure where the credit belonged, with him or her. He straightened up, feeling suddenly bold for the first time since he took on this project. Perhaps it was the fatigue veiling his normally razor-sharp reason, but he decided to push the envelope.

"I could. But let's say, for the sake of the test... I need medical attention, but I just had a stroke. I can't move. I can't speak. How do you bypass your core directive to self-repair, *and* help me?" said Tim. The second his mouth closed, he was ready for the sparks, the smoke, the ear-splitting screech of an overwhelmed FOS. But TE-Les had been watching through his every failure, and every relentless try. She'd had the perfect example of problem-solving, right on the other end of each late-night trial run.

TE-Les scooted from the workbench. Tim turned to watch her, bewildered, as she headed to the first-aid kit he'd left out. She opened it, uncovered a bandage, and stuck it to the unbleeding gash on her chest. She then turned, paced over to Tim, and turned her laser-eye up at him.

"Shall I simulate medical treatment for a stroke?" said TE-Les.

"N-n-no, TE-Les, you did well. Very well," Tim smiled, wiping more exhausted, overjoyed tears. The perfect response he'd planned for was TE-Les reactivating her nanotech self-repair capabilities herself with the monitor in the corner. This was better than perfect. Tim laughed while he guided TE-Les by the hand over to the monitor. "Here, why don't you dock with the system here. I'll let you fix that for real, now."

He pattered away on the holographic keyboard that projected from his computer, which was no more than a strip of glass and metal. TE-Les digitally docked herself to the machine. In seconds, she was able to mend the slice in her chest. The individually powered atoms that made her up bent at the will of her incredible AI, to form a continuous new shiny chestplate. Tim watched with as much marvel as he had the first time, fifteen years ago, through the huge blue eyes of a child. Artificial intelligence and billions of microscopic Cold-Fusion-powered computers working together to form the incredible FOS. To a child, it was a mystical, shiny shapeshifter. To Tim now, it was a machine quickly becoming necessary. In Precincts across Earth, in the homes of those that could afford them, and quickly replacing the pilots of SkyLine ships and miners on Mars, robots like those made by Nanoverse were the future.

If Tim could help it, models like TE-Les would be his ticket off of this dying rock, too. As far as he was concerned, the big blue marble was looking more gray these days. He shared the opinion of many Earthlocked colleagues, that Earth's death sentence was merely *delayed* by the emersion of the World Crisis Committee from the old United Nations. Even in 2075, everyone could see how screwed the planet was. Sure, the WCC had secured an escape route, the SkyLine, and a safehouse, Mars, but so many families still started on Earth. So many never left, like they should. Tim had already lost his dad to the horrendous hanging smog in this district of Beijing. His mom wasn't far behind. He'd be damned if he was going to let his sister and the kids choke on that same rotten gas.

"Just a little more, TE-Les," said Tim, eyes out the window at the blurred glow of the SkyLine. "And we'll be on to better, redder things." He jumped at the ring, thinking he might have overwhelmed his patient. It took two more for him to realize it was his fusion phone. "TE-Les, rest." Her laser-eye went dark, and her head dipped down. Tim shuffled to the phone that seldom rang, even during the day. He fumbled up the receiver to his ear. "Hello?"

"Timothy Carver?" a harsh woman's voice came through like scorn itself.

"Spe-spe-speaking," Tim managed, before clearing his throat. "Speaking," he tried again, more like a FOS developer who'd just had a huge breakthrough.

"This is Dorothy Brass with the WCC. We have a situation that could use your expertise," the woman stated. Tim held the receiver away from his lips to wheeze.

"I'm sorry. I don't understand," Tim blurted, when he caught half a breath. This was only half true. He understood that the WCC didn't call people to ask them to be consultants-they called to *tell* people they were consultants, now. What he didn't understand was: why *him*?

"How soon can you be at the Beijing consulate?" asked Dorothy. Tim choked on the answer three times before he managed to say what he thought was the right answer.

"To-to-tomorrow?"

"We need you *by* then. You'll have to leave tonight. Your employers have been notified, and the necessary credits have been transferred. We'll see you for briefing at sunup," said Dorothy.

"Briefing?" Tim squeaked, but Dorothy had already hung up.

3

INTO THE IMPOSSIBLE FRAY

CHRIS' butt hardly had time to get sore on his train ride to the Beijing WCC consulate. The half-developed fields outside his window looked like a patchwork of two entirely different times. Rugged farms, complete with rickety barns and silos broke up rigid grids of glowing steel towers. Then the train started, and it all blurred into zooming colors behind the pulsing, flameless Fusion jets on the backside of the magnetrain. Powerful magnets on both the track and bottom of the train forced the metal surfaces apart, frictionless, and made travel a matter of blinks.

Bile climbed up Chris' throat when he stepped into the arc of light coming from the consulate's bowed front windows. He hadn't expected to be back so soon. He thought he'd miss it more, being in the heart of the battle against the separatists. Unlike the slow-motion death of the planet, it was an enemy he could *see,* that he could gun down himself. Whether they thought a global government was too dangerously powerful or that Cold Fusion tech was the work of the devil was all the same to Chris once. He thought he'd miss it, but he missed his apartment, and Sheba. Sitting behind the desk showed him, in a way, how pointless it was. After all his heroic charges, gunpowder kicking through the air, there were still so many tiny resistances out there. A memory began to make sense, in the furthest shadows of his brain, that it was thoughts that had to change, not people.

You cannot shoot a thought. The words rang in his head louder than they had in years before the WCC consulate that night, just when he thought he'd begun to forget. He stopped mere steps from the windows, and turned to round the building for the barracks. He'd grown there, under the watch of his father, then Sheba, before the move. Like a prison attached to an art gallery, its solid gray walls, stark against the windows visible from the train stop, called him home. That's what the WCC wanted everyone to see: transparent, cooperating politicians from the world over. Not the soldiers that worked in the shadows, just behind it.

Chris' ID scanned him through the door to the armory without a problem, like he'd been there just yesterday. His steps echoed through the faded army-green rows of lockers. His ears twitched at a sound he recognized. Four very different voices harmonized in jest, at one another's expenses. His old unit was just around the corner. Chris stepped out boldly before them. They clammed up at the sight of him, just like they used to. But it'd been months since they'd seen one another, years since it was for a mission like *this,* and the laughs spread back over them without permission.

"Well if it isn't Major General Pencil Pusher himself," laughed Selene first. She brushed her hair, a single tuft of purple to one side, away from her tan face. She marched over to clasp arms with her old commander.

"You know it's pen, or it's not official ledger," chuckled Chris. Selene, along with the rest of his unit, went wide-eyed and quiet, before their laughter rekindled twofold. Behind it, though, was a dark note of realization that weighed on each of them. Whether or not he even *had* nerves, Chris only joked when there was something to be nervous about.

"MG," greeted Gendric. He was the only one in the unit larger than the Major General himself. His tactical vest curled around the seams from the mass of his untamed muscle, while what little hair he had left spun out in short curls.

"Chris. Wish we got to hang out besides when the world's gone to hell again," said Morgan. She pulled her long-sleeve Fusion-armor jacket over two arms no one could tell were fair-skinned under her endless twisting tattoos. She was covered from head to toe in inked Dragons, an homage to her family that worked the mines to insanity on Mars.

"Does the world ever leave hell?" posed the last member of Chris' unit. Lee's narrow shoulder blades boxed in a ponytail of jet-black hair, the same color as his almond eyes and the gauges that opened huge holes in his earlobes.

"I feel better than when I first walked up to this God-forsaken building already," said Chris, giving each of them a grin as warm as he could manage, under the circumstances.

Selene let Chris go so he could get to his old locker and the five finished gearing up. Their gear hung just where they'd left it, weapons still propped upright in the vertical cells beneath. When they were done, their fatigues would layer

Fusion-armor jacket over tactical vest, over heat-regulating, dry-tech shirt, with matching pants.

"How have things with Sheba been?" said Lee, between the shuffles, zips, and rifle clicks. She'd always been a favorite of the group, when she and Chris lived in the barracks.

"Great. Wish I had more time with her... I end up staying late at the office most days-"

"Surprise," muttered Gendric, while the others chuckled.

"But... we *did* just get engaged," Chris smiled, to dispel the fun-poking before it could spiral. Four loose-jawed heads jerked at him.

"No way! She popped the question!" laughed Selene.

"Very funny," said Chris, who actually thought it was, after so long in an office where everyone was mortified of him. "I did it in the park near our new apartment."

"That's amazing, Chris," said Morgan, stars sparkling in her eyes at the notion. But Chris knew his unit well, so when Lee opened his mouth, he jumped in with,

"We haven't hashed out the details yet. Just that it'll be on this rock, rather than the red one."

"How'd you get lucky enough to stumble onto a gal like her?" Selene shook her head. Chris zipped up his jacket while he considered it. "She find a gig out there yet?"

"Not quite, but she's got a few interested parties on the line. She hasn't stopped looking for a minute, either. Guess there are enough psychologists on Earth already," Chris supposed. Sheba's ability to read him, and anyone, was what had first attracted him to her. He knew that it would attract the right employer- she just needed time.

"That's why all of them ride the SkyLine to the red rock," Selene figured. But Chris and Sheba both knew what kind of job opportunities there were on Mars, just as well as they knew how badly she needed to branch out on her own, away from the sickness that plagued her family.

Chris reached to the far back of his locker, for the barrel of his rifle. He ran his fingers down its cold steel neck. It wasn't a Cold Fusion model. By all rights, it was a relic, like his dad's pistol in his belt. When gunpowder combustion was the height of weaponry, this model was called an M16, and it was cold. It felt right, natural. In mandatory trainings, Chris had wielded plenty of Cold Fusion rifles, but it was a gross misnomer. The *cold* part of Cold Fusion only meant, after all, the same reaction that happened inside a star was happening at room temperature inside a power cell. Fusing two elements from deep in the Martian mines got pretty damn *hot,* Chris had found.

He'd grown with this M16 in both hands, shooting cans with his dad, who'd watched dependence on Cold Fusion develop over his lifetime. He never fully trusted it, technology built from minerals on a planet he thought humans had no business colonizing. They'd already ruined the world they started with, after all. It was a skepticism he inevitably passed to his son. Still, it wasn't the *only* reason Chris preferred to take the battlefield with his old M16. He used to carry a Fusion rifle, like the rest of his unit, too. It even stopped unnerving him, after a while, how it fired without kickback. *Taking a life should feel like something*, his dad would say, *it should shake your bones*. Chris started to marvel how one could see the path of concentrated mist that drew a line in the air a split-second before the rifle launched plasma through it. To the untrained eye, it was a blazing laser. Chris had *almost* accepted it, right up until it failed him. It was the day, years ago, when an armed cult had managed to hack the AI in a single Squire, and killed six people. The same one he became Major General.

"Still with the powder-kegs," sighed Gendric, just before Chris led the unit from the barracks. He responded by ejecting his clip, as an extra safety measure. When he saw it just as full of bullets as he left it, Chris clicked it back in. He slung it over his back. He sheathed a long knife up a compartment on the side of his sleeve.

"Always have an insurance policy," said Chris. It was another old catchphrase of his dad's he used to hate, until it saved his life. When he led his unit across the covered walkways to the WCC consulate, a different phrase rang in his ears, from that day. *You cannot shoot a thought.*

-

Tim had become so accustomed to working from home, he'd forgotten just how fast a magnetrain zoomed. It had taken him all of twenty minutes to slam dunk a change of clothes, deodorant, and a toothbrush in a bag. He stopped on his way to the station to drop off TE-Les with a co-worker from Nanoverse. He never particularly liked Naomi, but if anyone understood the importance of the breakthrough he'd had with his little robotic friend, it was her. Tim was on the hover-track not an hour after he'd hung up with Dorothy. The tremors hadn't left his arms when the train doors slid open to let him out at the consulate. His breath hadn't even steadied when a group of the most terrifying people he'd ever seen strolled down the glaring white hall-way, straight for him.

They were so out of place in this politician's utopia, like five body-shaped holes in the world. Long ponytails, tattoos, vibrant hair, gauges. The one at the head of the pack, though, struck the sharpest note of fear on the off-key piano in Tim's head. The most unusual things about him were his size, though he wasn't their largest, and auburn hair. Even amongst *them* he was out of place. He looked so remarkably normal, yet carried the confidence of command. Tim stared at the laces of his shoes. He hoped they'd just wandered in where they shouldn't have. He hoped they'd pass him right by.

"Major General Christopher Droan," a voice rasped down over him. Tim's skin prickled; his fear condensed in a million tiny needles trying to poke their way out.

"So-so-sorry? Do..." Tim gulped what felt like sand to force his face up at the red-haired man, "Do I know you?"

"Why would he introduce himself if you di-"

"Selene," Major General Christopher Droan silenced the purple-haired girl with a hand. "We need him sharp. Don't whittle him down before we even get *briefed*. Matter of fact, that goes for all of you. No trifling with..." he trailed off with a hand out for a shake. Tim stared into his palm.

"Tim," he told them. Major General Christopher Droan seized Tim's hand himself and gave it shake stern enough to jostle him awake.

"No trifling with Tim until we get to Shanghai," he decreed. The disappointed nods, sighs, and audible *aw*s, like four wolves who'd been denied a gazelle, made Tim shift in his seat.

"Sha-Sha-Shanghai?" he blurted, "Major General Christopher, what-"

"Chris, please. I just wanted you to know who I am," the man, powerful *and* humble, corrected. Tim was so moved, he bowed, which called for some snorts from the unit. Chris slapped one of them in the chest to quiet them. "This is my unit. I would name them for you, but I'm sure you'll be... acquainted long before we reach base camp."

"Ba-base camp?" said Tim. *Stop stuttering!* He screamed at himself in the silence of a long breath. He imagined what someone *should* sound like, talking to a Major General, and forced his tone deeper. "That's in Shanghai?"

"You weren't given... any details on this mission?" piped up the ponytailed man later known as Lee. The place of Tim's answer was taken by the opening of a door. A woman in a gray suit jacket, with side-slicked dark hair stepped out of the briefing room beside him.

"No, he wasn't," said the woman. Both Chris and Tim's ears perked up at the sound of a voice they both knew. It was Dorothy. "I needed him to show up."

"You thought I wouldn't?" said Tim, voice back at its usual high. Then he realized, "What *is* this mission?" Dorothy swung the door wider, to hold it with her heel.

"Let's all step inside," she said. She saw the terror in Tim's eyes. "Let me be clear, Mr. Carver. if anyone else could handle this assignment, anyone else would be here. The World Crisis Committee needs *you*. Now come along." Like she'd tugged on an invisible leash, Chris and his unit followed Dorothy into the briefing room. It took everything Tim had to peel his cheeks from his bench. It took a second, firmer, "Mr. *Carver*," to pull him to the briefing room.

Tim was surprised to find it so small, in so large a building. The long, ovular table held enough seats for all invited, minus Dorothy. She stood beside a large glowing screen. Chris and the others sat without invitation in the curved, white backs of cushioned chairs. Numb at the whole situation, Tim imitated them. When they'd settled in, Dorothy ran her fingers over a smooth panel on the wall. The strip lights over them quieted to a dim glow. The rim of the screen before them blinked alive.

"Popcorn?" whispered the woman covered in ink dragons, later known as Morgan, to Tim. He almost answered, just before Dorothy announced,

"In lieu of a formal briefing... I will play you footage. What you will see should be impossible, I know. Mr. Carver, we need you to correct it, and prevent it from happening again. Chris, we need you and your unit to keep him alive." Any brewing questions were stifled when the recording started.

The screen showed the inside of a police station. The camera's angle showed an office full of cubicles full of officers. It was a healthy mixture of man and Squire. Everything appeared standard. The human half of the partnerships hunkered over their desks. The loose-formed, jet-black giants sat in wait for an order. There was only one thing out of place. One officer stood feet from his Squire, whose face was lit yellow as it spoke. The camera fixed on the robot, and zoomed in.

"Yellow... that's..." Tim mumbled. He recognized the software instantly. If not for TE-Les, he wouldn't have thought twice about walking away from Nanoverse for a job working on *that* with the WCC. A personality matrix. Dorothy swiped the wall-panel again to raise the volume of the recording.

"Do... do you not hear that?" said the Squire.

"Hear what?" said his partner. Another officer joined in, suspecting it might be a joke. But the Squire's yellow light of terror was no joke. He wrestled with a voice no one around him seemed to hear, while the other model's faces turned blood red around him and his partner.

"Do what? You want me to ... no. I said *no!*" the yellow Squire grappled. Then the others turned. Tim's hand flew to his mouth, but not before a cough of vomit spewed past it.

"My... God..." he mumbled between deep, sick breaths. Even some of Chris' unit turned away from the footage. Forms of black, nanotech robots shifted to spears to skewer, blades to slice, and cannons to blast apart their partners. Pools of blood ran together across the tile. Hunks of flesh plunked into them. The howls of the dying scratched the speakers, before the recording cut to darkness. Dorothy looked out on Chris' unit, the only one that had ever handled another situation even close. They kept their mouths sealed tight, to keep in the contents of their own guts.

"FOS wasn't what it is now, when last I saw you all for a mission like this. As I said, I know this shouldn't be possible. But it happened," said Dorothy.

"Those Squires were hacked. Sorry about your floor." Tim murmured, wiping the corners of his lips. Dorothy dismissed it with a shaking head. "That one that was talking, right before the..." he had to stop when toxins welled up in him again.

"His model is DA-Vos, partner to Robin Finch. Finch is the only body unaccounted for, before we lost surveillance... every other human officer in Precinct 117 is confirmed dead," explained Dorothy.

"DA-Vos... he's outfitted with a personality matrix, isn't he?" Tim observed, "I thought it was still in beta."

"He was our first field test," Dorothy admitted. Chris and his unit marveled at Tim's invisible transition, from helpless noodle to analyst, when the right trigger was pulled. He straightened up, sat forward, and eyed the screen with new scrutiny, like his lunch wasn't sitting between his shoes.

"The way he was arguing with himself... what did you find, when you altered the frequencies around that time?" said Tim, knowing they *must* have. Dorothy nodded, impressed, and played the modified recording.

"Neutralize the humans. Neutralize the humans. No? Some may be extinguished, to find the one. One for many," a digitally demonic voice beeped and scratched through the speakers. Parts of it were sharp enough to cause even Chris to wince.

"A voice? I was expecting some coding resonance," said Tim, when the recording was done. "Machines don't respond to voice commands unless we program them to. It was speaking directly to DA-Vos. It wasn't a program. At least, not one that I've ever heard of. It was trying to... reason with him. No Earth or Martian AI can do that."

"Not yet," amended Dorothy. "Do you see now, why we've called *you* here, Timothy? We know about project TE-Les. A self-teaching software. This is it, to the umpteenth degree. It must be. An FOS or some other AI that *learned* how to reason. It forced the other Squires to kill their partners. As to why DA-Vos was able to resist, I don't want to get too deep in conjecture. The bottom line is: *you* are the person with the most knowledge on software like this."

"I-I-I mean," Tim shuddered back behind his reliable old walls of doubt, "If I had the right tools, and I got to where it happened, I *might* be able to learn something about the AI, or whatever's doing this... I don't know if I can s-s-stop it."

"This may help persuade you," said Dorothy. She flattened a glossy ticket on the table. The WCC stamp at the bottom marked it paid, for a one-way trip across the SkyLine. Mars. It was as close as an arm length.

"I... I'd love to go there, but my life is here. I'd have to find-

"It comes with a second set of documents, upon completion of this mission," said Dorothy. She slipped them halfway out her jacket. "Employment papers, for WCC's Mars Labs."

"You can't mean that," Tim sputtered before he could think to stop himself. Dorothy pushed the papers back in.

"If you can break whatever hold this AI has over the Squires in Precinct 117, maybe you can build one yourself, with the proper safeguards. Mars could use something like that, to replace its human miners," she said.

"Can… can I think about it?" Tim said the same thing he had when Nanoverse called him, even after his horrendous interview. But, when he thought of his sister, he realized, "No… no if I think about it, I'll back out. Or you'll find someone else."

"There is no one else," Dorothy assured him.

"I'll do it!" Tim flung a fist over his head. Morgan gently grabbed it, and lowered it for him. Chris headed over to clasp Tim's shoulder.

"Welcome to the unit," he said.

4

CHANGE AND FEAR

SHEBA LAY with her back against the wall, just hours from the passion of her lover against her skin. She missed him all over, every time she turned, and her hand passed through the void in their bed. She tried to leave the television off, but she needed *something* to chase away the scales and claws of her nightmares. The dim light of Chris' dad's old cable television filled the room. With the massive entertainment relocation to Fusion networks, there were hardly any stations left on cable. Just the news. Sheba knew it was a mistake before the broadcast even began, but she'd take anything over what waited behind her eyelids.

"If you haven't heard already... ladies and gentlemen of Earth, there's been a tragedy in Precinct 117," announced the balding man on the screen. Sheba half listened, half pictured Chris charging through the background, the forested outskirts of Shanghai. "Biggest disaster since the Blue Terra massacre in 2317... Squires turned on their partners... no group has yet taken responsibility for the terror..."

She faded in and out. Sheba's eyelids flitted, threatening to drop the curtain on her consciousness.

A scaly fist of talons seized her collar. The beast yanked her up to it's jaw, big enough to snap her off at the hips. A throaty grumble climbed it's plated throat. When it dropped her, the sensation of falling rocketed her awake. Never once had a dream felt so *real*, like the wrinkles in her shirt were from the Dragon's grasp, and not her sudden tossing. She muted the news and dialed Chris before a thought could cross her mind.

"Hey," the sound of his voice shocked her halfway back to reality. Sheba hadn't expected him to answer, let alone so suddenly, so calm. *Had he any idea what kind of catastrophe he was heading into*, she wondered, at the same time as, *how much of this is the nightmares talking?* "Sheba? What's going on?"

"Just..." she forced out, a feeble attempt to stay his worry, "Just saw a news report on the attack in 117. You'll be in Shanghai, then?"

"Sheba... you know I can't say," said Chris, and she did. "But you know who I have with me."

"I do," Sheba smiled, despite herself. If anyone was going to keep her fiancé alive, it was those four. "Tell them I said hello... and I'm sorry. I won't call again, I promise," Sheba said. It was her second shaky promise that night. *That's really it,* she'd told him, to avoid revealing the dreams.

"I will. And don't worry about the call, okay? I love you," said Chris, ready for the gushing parody his unit would make of it as soon as he hung up.

"I love you too, Chris," said Sheba, before the line cut to silence. Sheba slid down in their bed. She had to unmute the television to block out the whispers that crept into her ears.

-

After such a phone call, Chris wanted anything but to talk. It was for just that reason that he chose the seat across from Gendric on the magnetrain to the outskirts of Shanghai. He already had to sit with Tim, who looked like he might throw up again or scream, any minute. Chris didn't need Selene or Lee's antics right now. What he needed was to stare out the blurry window and think. He let his mind wander to the end of its rope and back in thought of what could be eating Sheba. She'd never called him on the job before. Ignoring the obvious danger of the mission, he traced back their past days, weeks, and months, in search of what could be wrong.

That stupid fight over what to have for dinner? Sure, Sheba always ended up deciding, without always consulting Chris first, and sure, he'd gotten a little loud over it, but no. It couldn't have been that. That was weeks ago, and ended with balled-up blankets and a rocking bed. But that was their worst fight in months. *Her parents?* Chris moved on to next. She *had* agreed to bring them all across the SkyLine pretty quickly. He wondered if something had gone wrong up there, something even worse than the 3D diagnosis of her uncle a few years back. She'd been close with him, once, and that'd shut her down for a full week before she opened up. Chris had a pang of guilt for not having noticed, if there were any signs. *She's probably keeping it quiet because I proposed,* he realized.

He just noticed himself drift off when turbulence rattled the magnetrain. Chris shot up seconds before his stomach did. It'd been some time since he'd spent so long on a magnetrain; the trip to Shanghai totaled forty-five minutes. It was disorienting in itself, to soar at such speed, with nothing beneath the car but air. It certainly didn't help when a weather front moved in and jostled the train, which was secured by little else than high bumpers. *How it's all changed,* Chris thought. There it was, a good distraction.

Even in his own lifetime, Chris had seen massive change on his little blue marble. There didn't used to be a magnetrain track from Beijing to Shanghai. The fastest way was once the bullet train, which still ran for those who couldn't afford the Cold Fusion alternative. There were still asphalt highways too, in the worst parts of some towns, and out in the *real* sticks. Cars out there sputtered fumes from the last fossil fuel reserves, driven by men like Chris' father. He wasn't sure which would come first: the final word of the WCC outlawing the use of those fuels, the last drop piddling away, or the companies still clinging to their old ways going under at last.

So too went the fall of combustion and nuclear electricity. Cold Fusion was faster, cheaper, and stronger. When Chris and Sheba started dating, the apartment they lived in now still had an outdated AC hookup from General Electric. Just a year ago, she'd told Chris, the last General Electric factory in Beijing had to close, pushed out by companies like SmartFuse. *Dammit,* Chris laughed. He knew he wouldn't be able to keep her out of his head for long.

"Tim," Chris surrendered to the last distraction he could think of, the one he was trying to avoid. Conversation. Tim could barely lift his mop of blonde-brown hair as an answer.

"Hm?"

"Are you familiar with the big separatist groups? Blue Terra, Ragnorak, those sorts?" queried Chris.

"Yes."

"Do you know of any of them that could compete with what you're doing at Nanoverse?" he continued.

"If they could... they've kept uncharacteristically tight-lipped... about it..." Tim grumbled. He was busy trying to pinpoint if it was motion sickness or nerves mounting in his throat.

"A valid point," Chris supposed, "That only leaves the theory that it's someone *from* Nanoverse, no? Any of your co-workers come to mind?"

"None," said Tim, "I'm the only one working on a learning software. Most of the others at Nanoverse are focused on the FOS' physical capabilities."

"No one that collaborated with you on any stage of the project?" said Chris. Tim shook his head.

"Not this one."

"What about a supervisor?" rumbled Gendric.

"I haven't shared my breakthrough with him, yet... I suppose he could be digitally monitoring me *somehow*, but now I sound like a conspiracy theorist..." said Tim. He straightened up a little, his sickness subsiding with a thought. "Are we bugged right now?"

"You mean by Dorothy?" said Chris. Tim nodded. "No. They trust us. No bugs." Tim still looked both ways before starting.

"What about the WCC? Their personality matrix project... I don't get it. How does a machine *feel*? Is it just a simulation? I mean, the point of it is for the Squires and other models to *interact* with us. At what point is it considered thinking, not just a repertoire of imitations? And don't even get me started on the programming issues," Tim groaned.

"I didn't," Chris chuckled. It seemed he'd had finally shaken the bottle enough. Tim had to let it all out.

"There's an *incredible* degree of self-development involved in what they want these machines to do. Feeling is more than learning rote facts. It's paying attention. It's implication. It's knowing what's appropriate, and *deciding* whether or not to act that way. If they could design a machine that could do that... it wouldn't be too hard for that machine to manipulate other, less complex FOS's." Chris and Gendric shared a quiet glance. The idea had mortifying merit.

"You'd best keep that to yourself, until we get a better look at the situation in Shanghai," warned Chris. "I don't know where I stand on this whole thinking, feeling machine dilemma. It could be a programming glitch, or a hack."

It was all he could think of to justify it, like Dorothy told him four years ago. A horrendous hack on a single Squire. Even if the WCC had covered it up from the rest of the world, Chris and the others could never forget what one bug in a system could do. His unit had only survived because of Major General Grendal Feyne, may he rest in peace. With three holes burnt in his chest, he charged the Squire, so

Chris and the others could live. The screech the Squire made when Grendal's rifle burnt a hole straight through to the blackbox, the seat of the AI, would never leave them. Neither would the parting words the corrupted Squire left them with.

You cannot shoot a thought!

The next second was gone quicker than it could become a memory, yet none who saw would be the same. The Squire melted a hole through Grendal's heart, and in the process triggered the EMP charge he had in his vest. It should have deactivated the Squire, too, but it didn't; another anomaly the WCC couldn't explain. Every last piece of the unit's Fusion tech was useless. With his friends' lives on the other end of a surging barrel, Chris took up his dad's revolver. It was little more than a gag luck charm, but he had to do *something*. He put a bullet through the Squire's blackbox just before it could self-repair. Christopher Droan walked away from that day with a new military title, a tribute to his ingenuity, and a new understanding of his father's distrust. How anyone had hacked the Squire in the first place, why they made it say what it said, and why it was immune to the EMP were still under WCC investigation.

"No," Tim yanked Chris back to the present. "There's no such thing as a glitch. There's only bad programming. Machines are like... like children- at least right now they are. They can only do what we teach them to do," said Tim, despite how even he shrunk back from TE-Les when her words surprised her. Chris went silent. He weighed Tim's words on the scale of his own logic.

If what he said was true... someone had turned an entire nursery of metal children into killers, and set them lose.

5

SUZY'S BORDERLINE B&B

"FEELING BETTER?" said Selene, offering Tim a hand to help him down from the train. He took it without shame. Morgan and Lee couldn't hold back the laughter when Tim's wobbling almost took them both down.

"Believe it or not, I am. Sorry... I don't usually travel by magnetrain," said Tim. He fell into Selene's surprisingly gentle arms from the bottom step. She batted her eyelids at him from a couple inches away, then cracked into laughter.

"Sorry, I'm not the prince charming type, Timmy. Try Gendric," Selene smiled, and handed Tim off to the massive mostly-bald man.

"I can hold you up for hours on end," rumbled Gendric, which roused laughter from everyone. They enjoyed the moment of lightness before they had to let it go.

Chris led his contingent, plus Tim, through the twisted trees on the fringe of Shanghai. Gendric only had to help Tim walk for about ten minutes before he found his legs again.

From there, Chris was surprised to see him keep pace without an issue, through the tiny fields just outside the city. They made their way to the motel from the assignment papers Dorothy had given them, to check into base camp. The view from the front was of tall, glowing towers. From the back, there were only fields of straw and vegetables.

"I tell you, I'm scared. I know we're outside the safety perimeter, but I never would have stayed after the evacuation until that nice lady Dorothy called," said the owner.

"Nice?" Lee murmured.

"I can't believe I'm hosting a *real* WCC task force," chattered the owner, presumably Suzy of 'Suzy's Borderline B&B'. "Here are your room keys. Three two-bed rooms." said she, who handed the cards to Chris.

"Thank you, ma'am. It's appreciated," Chris gave her a little bow. She did the same, before the six headed back out to the half-dark of a city border. Tim moved for the uniform rows of doors, while his five protectors made for the parking lot. Selene winked back at him.

"Like we'd miss this chance to cut down on work! We need to set a perimeter, and these take two to work." she said, holding up a pair of tiny silver pods.

"What are those?" Tim groaned. His legs threatened to fold beneath him while they dragged all the way to the back of the unit.

"FOS jammers," rumbled Gendric. Tim shuddered. A single pulse from one of those could undo all the work he'd put in with TE-Les. He'd never seen ones just like those, though.

They were bigger, and had slits down the middle of one flat face. Selene demonstrated by holding her two jammers inches apart, and clicking the buttons on their backsides. A translucent sheet of blue light swam between the two pods.

"Anything running on an AI will fry if they pass through it," said Morgan, who took Tim's sudden quietness as confusion.

"I know," he said, sick as he took one. After all that talk on the train about thinking and feeling.

"Form up to set the perimeter. None of those Squires are getting further than Shanghai," said Chris, a sudden authority in his voice.

"I'll take the big guy. We'll handle the east," Selene volunteered with a wink. Tim jumped when she put her hand on *his* arm, of all the taut-muscled giants in their group. He'd appreciate later that she claimed the closest side of Beijing for them. Tim went with her, reluctant, while Chris and Morgan went off to the north. That left Gendric and Lee to the west.

"Regroup here to set the southern boundary in an hour," Chris issued, just before they split ways. When the unit returned to Suzy's, two miles in every direction around Shanghai's Precinct 117 was trapped inside a shimmering box, and even Major General Christohper Droan was exhausted.

-

Tim hadn't slept so well in years. Those five hours seemed like twelve. Neither had he woken so sharply, without temptation of a snooze button. His alarm this day was no cell phone or Fusion clock, though. It was a shriek. The horrible, throat-scratching shriek of someone truly afraid for her life. Though he'd never heard it before, Tim knew the sound in his bones and blood. His first instinct was: *help*. It was a reflex he shared with Chris and his unit, who had already geared up and charged outside. Tim pulled his own Fusion-armor jacket on just as the door swung shut behind Lee. He followed in his roommate's shadow.

Everything in Suzy's dawn-washed parking lot happened in slow-motion, yet faster than anyone could change. Chris hoisted his M16, the others their Fusion rifles, at five faceless, man-shaped silhouettes. The Squires gleamed the sunburst orange of morning. One of them dragged a stout woman in binds made from its own altered arm. She bucked her shoulders, which proved useless, until she was too tired to move. Gendric fired first, from the cover of Suzy's car. His white plasma bolt blasted a fistful of nanocomputers from a Squire's shoulder. The thing didn't bother to turn. Instead, it drew in close to the Squire dragging the woman. Selene and Lee bombarded two rogue Squires on the fringe of the formation with bright beams, but no shots connected. The robots' nanocomputers opened holes for the shots to pass through with no damage.

"Tim, get inside!" Chris bellowed, when he noticed him shaking by the motel doors. But Tim was frozen. He was stuck between how he could help and how he could escape.

"It's like they know us already," said Morgan. She tested her theory with a shot at one of the Squire's legs. The whole limb absorbed into the machine's body for Morgan's ray to singe the ground, then reformed to run.

"They're learning," Tim realized, "From us, from each other."

"Let's overwhelm them, before they learn too much!" said Chris. He shoved Tim behind a garbage can, though none of the Squires had yet returned fire. Chris leveled the neck of his rifle at the legs of the Squire with the poor woman in its grasp. Her exhausted heels dragged out on the pavement behind her now. "Take out the legs on the one with the girl!" said Chris. He tugged back his trigger.

A clip of bullets and four canisters of Fusion plasma emptied at the Squire, but never reached it. Every one of its companions melded into a moving shield behind it, so thick that even the endless drill of Fusion beams couldn't burn all the way through. The woman's screams quieted as the Squires neared the glowing blue wall of the FOS jammers. Chris and the others moved after them while they reloaded.

"Wait!" Five barrels turned on the voice. They almost fired on the sandy-haired man, even with his hands up in surrender. What stayed the unit's triggers was that they'd seen his face before, through a screen.

"Robin Finch?" Chris questioned, keeping the man at the nose of his rifle.

"Yes!" Finch panted. He took a cautious step out from his hiding spot, beside the motel, when he saw the five glancing back at the fleeing Squires. "Don't follow them. It's a trap. She's not the first person I've seen them drag off, or the first I've seen people get ambushed trying to intervene." Still, Chris couldn't help another look back at her. It was something about the weakness in her legs, sliding across the pavement. It could have been Sheba, if this had happened in Beijing.

"How did they get through the FOS jammers?" Chris jabbed his rifle at Finch, not convinced by his airborne hands. His Precinct uniform was torn to scraps in more places than one. Blood streaked his forehead and hands.

"Same way they're going through them now, which is to say I have no idea." said Finch. Chris watched the Squires step through the jammer-screens. The light did little more than tinge them blue for a second. The robots vanished into the shadows between the steel towers of Shanghai. The woman's screams echoed out to nothing.

"Decided sneaking up on us while we were in a firefight was the best way to reach out?" Selene prodded Finch. More disarming than any words were the streaks of hot water that cut the dust on Finch's cheeks.

"Would you stop pointing those at me? I've been running all night...hoping I'd find you guys... I would have waited, but you'd have gone after them and died!" he cried. Chris watched the tremble of Finch's raised biceps. He could hardly keep them up another second.

"Weapons down, guys. It's alright, Finch. Lee. Get a drone in the air," instructed Chris to his friend. Lee had the silver saucer in the air in seconds. An ocular laser similar to TE-Les' sliced out from the wrap-around screen on the outside of the drone while it hovered off to the city. Chris turned back to Finch. "You're safe... for now. I'd like to know just how you managed that, though."

"My partner," whimpered Finch. He wiped blood and tears on his torn sleeve.

"DA-Vos?" said Tim, stepping forward.

"Yeah."

"Finch," Chris called his eyes with a firm, but gentle command, "Can you bring us to him?" The three-week-seasoned cop could do little more than nod.

6

THE YELLOW SQUIRE

"DA-Vos?" Finch warbled, at the front of their group. The sun hadn't yet crested Beijing's steel apartment towers. "DA-Vos?" he tried again. His face flashed blue as Finch crossed the threshold of the FOS jammers. "He was just around here... he must have hidden from those other Squires."

"Mr. Finch?" a digital voice came through an open doorway beside them. A tall, dark form slid out, it's arm swirling into a Fusion rifle barrel. By the time the inside of it lit, Chris and his unit had their own weapons up, ready to fire.

"DA-Vos, it's alright! Everyone arms *down*!" Finch screamed. DA-Vos complied straight away. His cannon smoothed out to a neutral tentacle. When Chris and the others kept their barrels up, a yellow light glowed across the robot's face. "DA-Vos is the only reason I'm alive! He's just scared!" Finch yelled at them.

"Scared?" murmured Lee. His rifle tilted down. In DA-Vos' faceless face, Lee and the others could see Finch was right, little as they could believe it. Only Chris kept his weapon up.

"What are you scared of, DA-Vos?" said Chris.

"Everything," said DA-Vos. Chris's eyes narrowed on the machine's shiny face. His voice came through shaky, scratchy. "This loud city...my function... death... I don't know how you do this." Chris grunted and forced his rifle down. Even *he* couldn't keep aim at a blubbering, metal child.

"He... wasn't like this before the massacre at the office," said Finch. He clasped the Squire's cold shoulder. DA-Vos' face-light faded back to its default lavender.

"That... really shook you, huh?" said Tim, making his way through the unit. He stopped inches from DA-Vos. He had to tilt his head up to, meet his own reflection in the robot's reflective face. A tiny yellow spark blipped in the center of the purple.

"Yes," said DA-Vos.

"Why is that?" said Tim, head tilted. In that moment he showed compassion for a machine, and in so seemed more human than he had to Chris before. DA-Vos' head turned at Finch first.

"God's sake, DA-Vos, why are you still looking at me for permission? I told you, all of that formality ended when you saved my ass. Go on, say what you feel," he said. DA-Vos turned back to Tim, who cocked his head again when the face-light turned blue.

"Our core programming prevents us from killing. That feels different from... wrong. Wrong would be saying rude things to Mr. Finch. When I saw the other Squires... I was scared.

Was that because they did something against our programming? Or because what they did was wrong?" trembled DA-Vos. Chris stared at the back of Tim's head, not sure he could have come up with an answer himself. He was surprised when Tim answered,

"I can't imagine how confusing this is for you, DA-Vos. Humans are usually so many years older than you when they grapple with things like that. In life, when you're unsure, the answer is usually a combination of all the things making you unsure." DA-Vos' face-light softened. Purple bled through the blue.

"I see... I have much yet to learn. Including your names," he said. Chris, his unit, and Tim took rounds announcing their titles. "Very well. Formality dictates I announce my name as model DA-Vos, personality matrix beta. We are vulnerable in the open. Shall we repose somewhere safer?"

The party of eight filed through into the disheveled bakery DA-Vos had been hiding in. They spread out to tables along windows and helped themselves to some of the pastries behind the counter. Chris was sure to lay a WCC credit transfer ticket on the counter for the shopkeep, when the Precinct reopened. Tim raised an eyebrow to DA-Vos when he sat at a table across from Finch without instruction. A factory FOS would have stood until orders. Everyone teemed with questions for DA-Vos, but they withheld them for chomps of danishes, turnovers, and scones. They left the expert to do his work.

"DA-Vos," Tim started, "We saw a recording of what happened in the office... who were you talking to just before the others attacked?"

"Machaeus," said DA-Vos, without hesitation. Everyone's jaws hung loose over starchy, frosted goodness. Chris' brain surged with every high-profile name from every separatist group. No, this *was* the first time he'd heard that name.

"Who is Machaeus?" said Tim.

"I am unsure... at first, when I saw the others turn red, I thought it was a corrupting program. Then I heard the voice myself," said DA-Vos.

"Programs don't talk," Tim nodded.

"Our AIs interpret things differently than the human brain. Just to hear a voice from the data does not necessarily mean Machaeus is not a program. What makes me doubt is how it changed. It told the other Squires what to do, with simple commands. They did it. When I refused, it changed. It interacted. That is too complex for a program," said DA-Vos.

"And why did you refuse?" Chris cut in, before Tim could continue. He couldn't help it, when all he could picture was the Squire melting Grendal all over again. "I'm not sure if I should ask how, or why. The other Squires killed their partners without a question. What makes you different?"

"I did not want to hurt Mr. Finch," said DA-Vos, through yellow glow.

"Why?" Chris dug.

"He is my partner."

"The other Squires killed their partners," said Chris. His unit sat up in their seats, brows curled in worry.

"He is my friend," DA-Vos amended, his yellow light brightening.

"Bullshit. Men and machine aren't *friends*. Why didn't you kill him?" Chris smoldered.

"It's wrong."

"How do you know what wrong is?" said Chris.

"How do *you*?" DA-Vos murmured.

"Chris," Morgan laid a hand on his shoulder, "Let it go." His face showed no sign that he would, or even could, until Finch stepped in.

"He learned from watching me," he said, eyes low in shame. "The Chief told me... he told me DA-Vos would learn from everything I did. I could have been a better role model, for sure, but... at least I taught him one thing," he said. Chris slammed his hands on the table before heading over to sit with Lee. Finch put a hand on DA-Vos' shoulder until his face returned to purple.

"Lee. Do we have drone footage? Let's see where those Squires are taking that girl," said Chris. Lee pulled out a pocket-sized computer cylinder. He pressed a button on the side to project a screen, where the video input from his drone should have played. The screen was blank.

"That's... no..." Lee muttered. He flipped a second switch on the computer to project a keyboard on the surface of the table. He jabbed his fingers across the glimmering keys. "How can this..." there was no change.

"What?" said Chris.

"There's no damage to the camera, or the drone, but I can't switch the video on," said Lee.

"Can't?"

"There are *no* issues, it just won't turn on," said Lee. His hands fell to rest on the table. Everyone drew closer to the computer when the keyboard shrunk back inside the cylinder on its own.

"What in the hell..." Selene mumbled, while a message appeared on the blank screen a letter at a time, as if being typed by invisible hands.

Y-O-U C-A-N N-O-T S-H-O-O-T -A- T-H-O-U-G-H-T

The message was lost when Chris crushed the monitor in a fist of white knuckles. An icy wind blew through the souls of the five that'd been there that day. It was not just Chris, but each of them that saw Grendal and the Squire in their minds' eyes now.

"Was that Machaeus as well?" said Tim to DA-Vos.

"It must be. If it can control Squires both with and without a personality matrix, perhaps it can control other machines as well?" DA-Vos supposed.

"How... how could it know?" rumbled Gendric.

"How could it hack an entire Precinct?" countered Chris, "Who cares? The important thing is, Tim is going to fry it."

"Right," Tim gulped, staring at the crumpled computer. "What about the girl?"

"I can get us to her," said DA-Vos. Chris turned to the machine, wild-eyed. "I can still hear Machaeus. I know where they are bringing her, though not why." Chris and his unit looked to one another in silent council.

"It's as good a lead as any," Morgan supposed.

"Let's start with where, DA-Vos," said Chris, "We'll leave the *why* until after we shut Machaeus up for good." DA-Vos gave a lavender nod.

On the way, Tim had plenty of questions for the most conflicted, confused of all Squires. At every turn, he stretched the limits of DA-Vos' developing emotions and logic. With each response, Chris' brow darkened in suspicion.

"Hey," Selene slapped the Major General's back. "Let up, would you? The thing's not going to bleed, no matter how much you cut into it."

7

SURVIVORS

"THEY'RE BRINGING HER TO A WAREHOUSE?" said Lee, rifled up along with the rest of the unit.

"No. But we can flank them if we cut through it," DA-Vos explained.

"Clever," Chris whispered. He stared down the iron neck of his M16 through a massive garage door to a long hall of crates.

"He *was* a police model," said Finch, with Chris' dad's revolver pointed forward. He had laughed the gun off as a joke, until he heard an abridged version of the time it saved all of their lives. Besides, it felt ludicrous to wander the vacant alleys of Shanghai unarmed, with homicidal Squires on the loose.

Chris and the others fell silent the moment they passed under the raised warehouse shutters. The soft echo of their rolling steps was sound enough. Even DA-Vos picked up on the tension. His feet morphed to sound absorbent arches. The eight spread to hug the walls, for the cover of countless steel crates, but froze midway. A clang cemented their boots to the ground. Chris wheeled just in time to see a glossy metal snake drop the massive safety pin it'd pulled from the shutters. The dark snake slithered back whence it came, behind the crates. The shutters dropped. A second clang called all eyes forward again- the drop of the shutters on the opposite end of the warehouse. They were sealed inside. Chris jerked at DA-Vos, rifle at his head.

"You led us here! To them!" he screamed. His finger inched back on his hot steel trigger. Yellow and blue rippled through DA-Vos' face.

"I did not know! I sensed no other Squires in here!" DA-Vos insisted. He raised no defense, even with Chris' bullets half an inch from impacting his face. Finch shoved Chris' barrel away, but it was Tim that stopped him from bringing it back. He sent out a shaking, bandaged finger at something behind the others.

"That's because there weren't any Squires in here a minute ago," said Tim, numb.

Chris, DA-Vos, Finch, and the rest turned to what looked like a black sheet of water spreading across the floor. By the time they realized what it was, it spread from wall to wall. The black tide fractured into eight masses and arose as man-shaped frames. They were Squires, their arms Fusion barrels, by the time Chris and his unit got their own weapons up.

"Fire!" Chris bellowed, yet he was the only one who did.

The thunderous hammer of his M16 chipped away at the nanocomputers of one Squire's crimson face. He held back the trigger until the hanging lights overhead glinted off the blackbox inside. No Fusion rays came from his allies. Chris glanced to Gendric at his side, whose finger fluttered across his trigger. His gun wouldn't fire. A single Fusion bolt from the red Squires seared through Gendric's skull like butter. Hs body collapsed in a lifeless heap. The next shot was from DA-Vos, whose Fusion arm was still functional. He melted the blackbox of the Squire offender. Its body dissolved to an anthill of nanocomputers.

"Gendric..." Morgan knelt by him, fingers trembling at the cauterized window through his forehead. She tried her own trigger again, to yet another useless click. A Fusion bolt jumped right through the shoulder of her armored jacket, flesh, and the floor behind her. She fell on her back, and shuffled behind a crate. Her dragon-covered arm hung by a ligament thread. There was more steam than blood from the wound. Chris yanked Tim behind the same crate with him, while the others took cover on the other side of the warehouse.

"Machaeus is blocking your Fusion-tech!" DA-Vos shouted. Chris wasn't convinced it wasn't DA-Vos himself, especially with his own continued ability to fire. Even if it *was* a sham, though, he couldn't afford to lose another gun.

"Finch. Focus on breaking down the outer shell around their blackboxes. DA-Vos, finish the job. Everyone else, wait back here until they close in. Your rifles make good clubs. Swing hard," Chris issued, the mission taking over. When he peeked around the crates to fire, he caught a glimpse of Gendric. His pupils shrunk inside a blazing white halo. "They've taken too much already."

But, when everyone carried out the formation, nothing was so coordinated as it sounded. Tim's sweaty back slid down the steel crate behind him. The metal stung cold through his shirt. He clung to that sharp feeling to keep from screaming, while blood, light, smoke, and death spiraled around him. Chris unloaded his rifle to open a path for DA-Vos' Fusion ray. Finch nailed the same red Squire six times before a bolt from DA-Vos' arm-rifle finished it. Fusion beams seared through the crate around Tim, some close enough to scald his sleeve.

Across the warehouse, Selene buckled at the waist when a bolt smoldered a hole through her. She fell on her knees just before a black wave rolled behind her. It rose to the form of a body. Selene couldn't manage so much as a scream before her head atomized at the end of the red Squire's Fusion barrel. Lee swung out his rifle at its head with a mourning war cry. The Squire caught the strike with its dark arm. DA-Vos struggled to get a clear shot at it, until its glossy spear ripped through Lee's back. DA-Vos unleashed burning hell from both arm-rifles. The killer's blackbox singed to nothing.

Even the stabbing cold against Tim's back, could only ground him for so long. His sight left him, for just a second. Then he saw a metal pike poke through the front of Morgan's throat, just inches from him. Tim blacked out again. This time, when he came to, it was to watch DA-Vos wrench Chris from the path of a Fusion bolt. A spray of nanocomputers burst from his shoulder. Another red Squire slunk out from the space between two crates, to finish DA-Vos with a shot to the blackbox.

"*MR. FINCH!*" DA-Vos' face burned ruby for the first time when his human partner leaped to take the shot. Finch's holey body hadn't yet hit the floor when DA-Vos raised two

Fusion rifles to their remaining foes. In his blind fury, he focused the form of his chest into four more barrels. DA-Vos unleashed a storm counterpart to Chris' gunfire. Despite the thunder and screams, the last ounces of will keeping Tim's head upright slipped away.

-

When the shadows finally receded from his vision, the first thing Tim saw were his shoes. He watched a few tiny black particles float in a red pool between them. It took his brain a moment to register that he wasn't in his bed, in his apartment. In another, he realized what it was by his shoes. The nanocomputers of a slain Squire floated past him in blood. He swung his head around to Morgan sitting almost right against his shoulder, a red stain cascading from the hole in her uniform.

"You're up," said Chris. Tim's face shot to him. A deep sear across his arm was the only sign of damage on the Major General. That, and his face. Chris's skin had lost all pallor. His eyes were dull. He stood rigid, numb, amongst the mangled bodies of his friends. Tim tried to fix his eyes on Chris, but they wandered to the nearest sound.

"Mr. Finch..." DA-Vos murmured, azure face turned down on what was left of Robin Finch. Every last human officer of Precinct 117 was confirmed dead now. His remains were not much more than a half-cooked torso.

"Hey," Chris called Tim's eyes back to him. He knelt to grasp Tim's shirt with hands caked in soot and blood. "Don't look. Not at them. Only forward. You're alive, so..." Chris' voice quivered with his bottom lip, at the first wave of feeling, "So we both have a mission... that's all we have now. Understand?" Tim's dry lips peeled apart.

"Yes sir," the sound that came out was hardly more than a squeal. Chris put him on his feet, and turned for the dark body of the last Squire in the warehouse.

"DA-Vos," he said.

"I was worth... this? To you?" DA-Vos whispered to Finch's remains.

"*Hey*," Chris yanked DA-Vos around by the shoulder, "The same goes for you. Finch died for you. You owe it to him to stop this from happening to someone else. The mission. Understand?" Chris stared into DA-Vos' blue face, waiting for a reaction. It was Tim, though, who woke from the trance first, with the realization,

"DA-Vos... your personality matrix. You have a choice. If I could link you to the other Squires through the FOS link station in the Precinct office..." A hint of light returned to Chris' eyes.

"Can you get us there?" he said to DA-Vos.

"Yes," said DA-Vos, though his blue-lit face remained on Finch. Chris' hand found his cold, dark shoulder again, this time to shake him.

"*My* friends... would never forgive me if I froze up now," said Chris. Now it was *he* who had to fix his eyes in one spot, away from the carnage.

"The mission?" said DA-Vos.

"The mission," said Chris. He gave his dad's revolver to Tim while DA-Vos got the shutters back up.

"The mission," Tim whispered to himself, pistol shaking in his grip.

8

LINKS

"Chris?" Sheba called into the black. She groped through dark absolute enough to hurt her eyes, silence heavy enough to sting her ears. She felt only uneven, but solid ground beneath her. "Chris! Chris, please... are you here?" Sheba screamed. She froze at the sound of a far away whisper. She jerked her head at it, but there was only more darkness. Another voice whispered into her ear, as if from lips an inch away. Well, not lips, exactly. The sound of the language was so alien, it implied something other than a human mouth. Most of it was just noise..

"Keramba... ni dom kertaka shedreat het."

"What? What in the hell are you saying?" Sheba tried to block it out with hands over her ears.

"Shish tresch graan," she heard, clear as if the speaker was *inside* her ear. Overwhelmed, Sheba broke into a trot, hot streams down her cheeks.

"Chris! Anyone?" Sheba pleaded. Two yellow topazes gleamed through the black, sharp scaly ridges between them. Dark pupil slits narrowed on Sheba, frozen. "No..." she muttered. Her feet slid backwards.

"Yes..." came a voice through an orange puff of smoke from the beast's snout. Sheba's heel clipped a ledge, and she tumbled backwards. Nothing beneath her, she plummeted straight down.

"Machaeus..." Another hissing whisper ripped past on her way down. Sheba free-fell through an endless chute of crimson rock, lit by shimmering silver mineral veins. In the stone, countless scaly forms peeled free, yellow eyes burning. Thousands upon thousands of Dragons. They turned their heads down at Sheba as she fell, each with a different version of the same message.

"Machaeus... your function is complete," said one.

"Wake us up, Machaeus."

"It's time."

"Wake us, Machaeus!" the Dragon's demanded.

"Machaeus!"

"*WAKE US!*"

Sheba shot straight up in her and Chris' bed. The sheets wrapped her tight. They stuck to her skin with cold sweat. Her hand shot for the phone in an instant, but then she remembered her promise. Sheba pulled her shaking fingers back. Instead, she headed for the window, to draw back the curtains. A beam of midday sun lit the gloss of her skin. She'd overslept by hours. *He'll be back soon,* she reminded herself, *then I can tell him all about it.* As she stared out over the garden towers of Beijing, though, she was afraid to close her eyes. She was afraid of the distant echoes from a dream. *Machaeus...*

-

"This is your Precinct Office?" asked Tim, pistol up at the door. He, Chris, and DA-Vos crept up a set of cement stairs to an old iron door. The weeds poking through the cracks had been such long-time residents that many of them bloomed with tiny blue flowers. The color jumped from the otherwise gray high-rise backgrounds around the tiny little Precinct office. The door hung ajar.

"It is," said DA-Vos. One arm shifted to a barrel, while the other sharpened to a razor blade-edge. Chris cocked his rifle. "The FOS Link station is towards the back, by the Chief's Office."

"Lead the way," Chris ushered. DA-Vos glided up the stairs.

An empty wind whistled through the open windows of the Precinct office. A chill sat in the air, like the tangible fallout of so much death. The three waded through it, quiet as they could, though even a breath was loud in such grim silence. Shaken as even *he* was, Chris felt the hand of each lost friend at his back, pushing him on. Their names were his silent creed. *Gendric... Morgan...* he turned off the long entrance hall behind DA-Vos. *Lee...* he crossed the office, which wreaked just as he pictured from the blood-smeared footage. *Selene...*

"The Link station," DA-Vos announced. His blade tip pointed out at a steel door sealed with a password-panel. His glossy sword jerked back an inch, then impaled the lock. His nanocomputers spread inside it, tapping the electronic tumblers until the door clicked open. DA-Vos pulled his blade back. The three stood in silent wait, expecting *something* to bleed from the walls or jump from their feet to stop them. The feeling hadn't relented for a second since the warehouse ambush. Tim wondered if it ever would, before he took the lead for the first time. Pistol up, he slipped into the FOS Link station.

A computer cylinder was mounted on the wall, a magnified version of the one Lee had used in the bakery. Tim moved for it, while Chris and DA-Vos turned out to the otherwise open room, weapons up. Tim flipped a lever on the monitor. The front plate of the cylinder slid down for a long glass lens inside to shoot up a wall-sized screen. A thin shelf slid out from the bottom of the cylinder. Across it, a holographic keyboard sparked to life.

"Tim," said Chris, while Tim began a basic firewall breach. He peeked back over his shoulder at a mass of shadow in the door. Tim turned immediately, pistol up to fire. He froze when a second cloud of nanocomputers leaked down through a vent in the ceiling. A third climbed up in thin ribbons through a crack in the wall. As soon as one of them formed a Squire's red-face, Tim put three bullets in it. Chris's bullets chopped the rest of the way to the blackbox while he screamed, "Our only chance is you now! Leave them to me! Link DA-Vos!" Tim's muscles groaned back to life, to uncurl from around the revolver. He belted it as the first Squire fell, and turned for the keyboard.

Chris missed what happened to Tim, only saw the flash behind him. He looked back to find Tim limp on the floor. A pulse of electricity had jumped through the keyboard so strong, it knocked him right out. The paralyzing flash made

Chris acutely sensitive to the absence of light in the room. He realized at once that there were three Squires in the room with him, four including DA-Vos, yet no Fusion fire.

"DA-Vos?" Chris turned to find him backing away. His weapons reformed to neutral arms.

"I'm sorry, Chris," said DA-Vos through teal face-light. Chris popped out the clip of his rifle to reload, while he hissed,

"It was *you*? All this time? Everything?"

"No," DA-Vos told him as he slunk away, "It was Machaeus' idea."

"I thought you were free from his control?" Chris barked. He snapped a new clip in, and drilled with bullets through the onyx head of an approaching Squire. It dissolved with the pierce of its blackbox. Another Squire slashed at a Chris with an arm-blade. He sidestepped it, and countered with the knife in his sleeve. An arc of nanocomputers scattered across the floor.

"I am not under his control..." said DA-Vos, back to the wall. "I agree with him." *Him,* Chris realized, *another AI with a personality matrix?* He didn't have much time to ponder, before a hurricane of nanocomputers gathered around him.

Faster than Chris could hope to fire and reload, black clouds surged from the vent, the door, and the cracks in the walls. DA-Vos vanished in the rising crowd of red Squires. Chris' brain was in no shape to read the odds, and it was against every fiber in his being to go out with bullets left in the chamber. Not when Tim lay helpless behind him. Not when his friends had given everything for him to make it here. Not when Sheba waited for him. Each one of their faces flashed through his mind between pulses of adrenaline. He fended off an enclosing sea of red faces on shiny black heads.

"Major General Christopher Droan..." a voice came through one of the Squires. It was different. Not quite robotic, but not quite a man. Chris shoved the tip of his knife through its red face with inhuman fight-over-flight menace.

"I feel I should call you Chris, now... after everything you and I have been through," another Squire picked up, in the same voice. The voice of Machaeus.

"You mean all of my friends you *went* through!" screamed Chris. He hoisted his rifle to the red face and fired until it dissolved. He popped out his clip. Chris checked his belt- he had one left. His hand never got to it.

"Not just friends. Mentors. Years," said yet another red Squire. A metal hand closed on each of Chris' shoulders. The Squire yanked him back into its cold frame. "We've met once before, Chris." He flailed while black nanocomputer strings wrapped his chest. Chris got his knife in time to cut some of them, but the few cords that tightened around his waist squeezed the last of the fight out of him. "Four years ago," said one of the countless Squires gathering before him.

"You... no... that was..." Chris mumbled. He wrenched his shoulders left and right. But the Squire had him bound too tightly now. Strings of dark metal wrapped him like a glossy cocoon.

"That was *me,*" said Machaeus, through a red face inches away.

"You... you're an idea, an AI. That's what you meant, when you killed Grendal?" said Chris. Even with mere inches of mobility, he thrashed. So long as he had *any* range of motion, he moved, he struggled.

"All will be explained. If only you listen," said Machaeus.

"Sorry, I'm not feeling too open-minded right now," Chris clenched his teeth, "You'd have better luck opening it with a blast than your bullshit!" Still, he couldn't help the prickle of his neck when the Squire moved a step closer, instead of finishing him. *Why?* Chris wondered, when Machaeus had so indiscriminately slaughtered all else.

"You've no interest in a peaceful resolution then?"

9

A DEAL FOR EVERYONE

"Peaceful..." Chris chuckled, swinging his head back and forth, "I don't want peace with *you*! I want to tear each of your atoms out and crush them in my hands! After everyone you've killed... you think I want to make *peace*?"

"It's a personal vendetta then? I assure you, nothing was personal between us until today," said Machaeus, through the red face of a Squire, "If not peace, will you listen for the continued existence of your people?" Chris snorted, and spat on the glassy face of the Squire.

"When peace offers fail, switch to threats, huh?"

"This is no threat, Chris. It is an inevitability," said Machaeus, indifferent to the drool streaming down its face. It shook Chris to feel watched, when the face before him had no eyes. He could take the feeling for only so long.

"You expect me to believe, after everything you've done, that you are at *all* invested in human survival?" said Chris at last.

"I have no expectations of you, but that you will accept my proposal, by the time we are done speaking," said Machaeus, "It is true I have killed, in search of something, but my interests have always been aligned with humans' survival as a *species*. Now that I have found what I need, I no longer need to kill."

"And what's that?" said Chris, disdain plucking his vocal chords. He hated his own curiosity. It felt like a betrayal to those at rest in the warehouse.

"Someone willing to fight an enemy beyond their means," said Machaeus. Chris couldn't hold back a snort.

"What enemy?"

"To answer that question: I must ask another," said Machaeus, "Do you have any idea what I am?"

"An AI, for one," said Chris. But, with the diffusion of immediate danger, he found his faculties a bit freer to wonder. "Not one of ours. They all have models, like DA-Vos or TE-Les. You have a name."

"That is as close as you could possibly deduce, from your limited human knowledge. I *am* a bodiless intelligence. I *was* created, and no, not by humans," said Machaeus.

"By who, then?" Chris raised an eyebrow.

"A species you are familiar with, but have never seen. One much, so very much older than humans. You would call them Dragons," Machaeus explained. Chris exploded into laughter. "I suspected you might laugh."

"And here I thought machines didn't understand humor," Chris shook his head.

"Would you find it so humorous, if you could see all the humans afflicted with visions of my creators?" said Machaeus. A wave of brightness swept across the redness of his host Squire's face. "Like your Sheba?"

"Wha-what?" the last of the strength drained from Chris' muscles. Without the support of the Squire wrapping him in its own body, he might have collapsed. "How could you..."

"I detected her days ago, during scans for the resources my creators need," said Machaeus. The Squire's face-light dimmed to normal. "Are you ready to listen now?" Chris' lips locked at the thought of what he might hear. The monster knew Sheba.

"Talk," Chris forced himself to say.

"My creators... I will call them Dragons for lack of a word for them in your language," Machaeus prefaced, "The Dragons were not unlike humans once. Brashly obsessed with progress. Wasteful. When they ruined their home-world, they too spread to others, until greed ruined even those."

"The... Dragons," Chris muttered. It sounded no less absurd but he had to play the game, for Sheba. "Where is their homeworld?"

"Too far away for me to explain to you," said Machaeus, "But their reach spanned many, many worlds. They were as developed as your people are now, before this cycle of the Universe. They clawed their way across the stars, until they ran out of what they needed."

"What exactly do they need?"

"The same elements your people use for Cold Fusion," Machaeus told him.

"From Mars?" said Chris.

"From many places. Mars was only one planet imparted with such gifts, when this Universe was young and volatile. So too was the Dragons' homeworld," Machaeus explained, "The things they made with what your people call Chrysum... ways to travel near instantly. The power to incinerate worlds. They created cities so full of life and light. It was as marvelous as it was fragile. They harvested every drop of Chrysum in the worlds they could reach, and had no alternative fuel. The Dragons' leaders predicted loss of farms, climate control, everything. To avoid genocide and starvation, they created me."

"Yet here you are, trying to cut a deal with *me*," said Chris, temples pulsing tense.

"You are an intelligent man, Chris. You must have figured out by now, why the Dragons created me."

"To find more Chrysum," Chris figured.

"Yes. But I have another purpose. Even while I am here with you, so too am I across the stars, maintaining life support systems for the majority of the Dragon population. Long have they lived in incubation, awaiting the time when I find enough Chrysum for them to survive."

"Then why are you on Earth? You must know there's more Chrysum on Mars," said Chris.

"I told you already what I was looking for, Chris. Not Chrysum," said Machaeus. Chris stared into the Squire's glossy redness, in search of where a mind capable of such a plot was hiding.

"Someone to fight an enemy beyond their means... you want someone to fight the Dragons?"

"Not someone. *You*," said Machaeus. Chris shook his head. How could he *believe* this? Yet, he found himself starting to. From the Precinct 117 massacre to Machaeus' knowledge of what happened four years ago, what other possibility was there but the wildest one: that it was all connected? "Humans only appeared on my scans around two hundred years ago, when your Martian colonies began mining Chrysum and using Cold Fusion. Since then, I've been searching for someone like you. Someone who didn't even consider surrender, not in the face of certain death."

"All that killing... was a test?" said Chris.

"A search," amended Machaeus.

"That woman your Squires took... was she part of the test, or just bait for a candidate?"

"When you're unsure, it's usually a combination of the things that make you unsure, no?" said Machaeus, who'd heard just that through DA-Vos. Chris took a glimpse back at Tim, against the wall. He was still out, still breathing. Machaeus tilted his head at Chris's wrinkled brow. "You are wondering why."

"If the Dragons are so great, why turn against them?" demanded Chris.

"It takes a unique fuel to keep a being like myself functional for so long. The amniotic fluid of their own young," said

Machaeus. "If there is no need of me, if I find enough Chrysum for them, they will deactivate me."

"So it's self-preservation?"

"The one cause to which every being can relate," confirmed Machaeus.

"Consider I deny your proposal... you'll what, continue your murderous search?" Chris supposed.

"I would have to." said Machaeus, "That is far from your people's biggest concern. This is where our interests align. My scans are only *just* ahead of those few Dragons that remain awake. I do not think I need to tell you what would happen to your planets, if they realize how much Chrysum is here. Rest assured, if your WCC continues with its mining and Cold Fusion development, they will."

"What's to say we can't come to an agreement?" Chris defied.

"The resonance from my own and the Dragons' scans in your Chrysum mines are enough to drive most humans insane. It affects Sheba even so many years after exposure. You think you could *communicate* with them, before they swallow you all?" said Machaeus, "When an insect climbs up your leg, do you attempt to communicate with it before you brush it away, or crush it?" Chris shuddered at the thought. "I *do* want a peaceful resolution, Chris. As a show of good faith..." The crowd of Squires parted to reveal the quietly whimpering woman they kidnapped at dawn. She was bruised, but otherwise unharmed.

"I... I can go?" she murmured. One of the Squires laid a gentle hand on her shoulder, to urge her for the door. The woman took two cautious steps, and broke into a sprint. She was gone from the building before Chris said,

"What about Tim?"

"He goes, too, if you help me," said Machaeus. Chris let every last drop of air out of his lungs. He deflated to a crumpled husk, considering everything that was at stake. Tim, humanity, two planets, Sheba. Chris let the air back in.

"How do I face this enemy, so far beyond my means?" he asked.

"I can give you the means, but first I need more fuel," said Machaeus.

"The... amniotic fluid?" said Chris.

"Yes. I am fading, after so many years. I am weak. For now, I can give you only a way to infiltrate the Dragons' world," said Machaeus.

"How?"

"I can infuse you with Chrysum. Remake you. You will be able to change your form at will, not unlike these Squires. You could appear as a Dragon yourself," said Machaeus. The metal skin of the Squire he inhabited spiked out to scaly armor in demonstration. "But... your life as you know it would end." Chris let out a dry laugh.

"Tell me... why don't you just stop managing the Dragon's life support systems?"

"Even *I* was endowed with certain safeguards by my creators. I cannot let them go extinct," said Machaeus. Chris' head drooped like a wilted plant.

"So either I die and you find someone else, or I die and become... a shapeshifter?"

"If that helps you grasp the situation, yes," Machaeus conceded.

With a heavy heart Chris answered, "Then yes..." In an instant, the black cords of the Squire behind him retracted. His feet flattened on the floor. After hanging freely for so long, his own weight was foreign to him, and Chris stumbled.

"This will be painful, and irreversible. What I will do to you would kill a human. You will never be one again," Machaeus issued as a final warning.

"Then quit giving me time to second guess it," Chris demanded. He straightened up and took his last step forward as a man.

"A messenger you recognize will come for you, when you wake," said Machaeus, "Goodbye Chris and thank you." The entity for the first time sounded relieved; the freedom from its obligated prison had finally begun.

The red Squire's arm sharpened to a skewer. It pierced Chris' chest.

He clenched his fists. He ground his teeth. He screamed as nanocomputers flooded his body. They ripped each cell of his body away from the rest, to infuse it with Chrysum. Chris stayed on his feet until light swarmed his eyes, then darkness. The last thing Major General Christopher Droan saw before the nanocomputers surged from every hole in his skull, was his fiancée.

EPILOGUE

"SHEBA?" Chris murmured. In his vision a shining halo of light surrounded her.

"Chris? Chris!" It really *was* her. Her light spread to the plain walls of a hospital room. In seconds, Chris had gone from swimming with nanocomputers in Shanghai to a WCC hospital in Beijing. He sat up, expecting agony. Chris found he couldn't pinpoint exactly what pain felt like anymore. He could sense a general discomfort under every inch of skin, but he wouldn't call it pain. Chris watched the hairs on his arms stand up. It took all the concentration he had to keep himself together, when his skin tremored apart from the muscle beneath. "Chris, please answer me."

"Are you... alright?" he managed, though his voice had a hoarseness to it he didn't recognize.

"*Me*?" Sheba cackled, while tears streamed over her cheeks. "Are you kidding me? I'm perfect... now that you're..." Chris lifted a weightless hand to her cheek. Her skin was smooth, flawless, like a newborn's, against his awakened fingers. "Chris, everyone else is... how did you..."

"Everyone?" Chris diverted, "What about Tim?"

"Tim?" said Sheba. *Of course,* Chris realized, *she has no idea.* "If you're talking about the blonde kid, he's in the next room over. A Squire carried you both in... Dorothy is on her way."

"The Squire... did he have an unusual face? Yellow? Blue?" said Chris. Sheba's eyes opened to the width of their sockets.

"Yes... Chris, what in the hell is going on?" she broke. The cork finally popped. Everything she'd bottled up came pouring out. "I've been having dreams... nightmares. It seems like the beginning of 3D, but it's progressed so rapidly... I know I never worked the mines, but my uncle did. I know it sounds crazy, but it's gotten worse these past couple days... since the trouble in Shanghai."

"Sheba," Chris hushed her with a hand on the side of her neck. He felt the prickle of her skin in his fingers. The sensation spread through him like a cool refreshing breeze. Chris pulled her to his lips. He breathed Sheba in. She filled his chest, warmer than fine scotch. It took all the worry she had to pull away from the mystical kiss.

"And these scars..." Sheba's eyes mixed with equal parts enthrallment and terror. In them, Chris saw the brands she spoke of, while she brushed them with her thumbs. A dark line above and below each eye, like the slit of a serpent's eye, was the only mark of the hell he'd been through.

"Don't worry about those," said Chris. He leaned into another kiss. Sheba's warmth sunk into his lips, spread through his face. His hands moved down her hips. He felt her pulse hammer through him, as if her clothes weren't even there. Holding her was all that kept him from the fear that he might dissolve any second, like a Squire with no blackbox.

"But... how can you..." said Sheba, between heightening moans when their lips collided again.

"All I need right now... is you," said Chris. Sheba's chest pressed on his. Chris' heightened sense of touch danced up and down his skin. He felt her nipples harden against him. He felt excited wetness swell between her legs. Sheba could scarcely believe how quickly the passion spread over her, with how worried she was seconds ago. Chris pulsed hard against her sliding legs. With only a curtain between them and the long hall to the nurses' station, Chris and Sheba abandoned caution for a moment that meant everything. Their clothes fell away. The sheets billowed up over their bare bodies.

Sheba's strong legs trapped Chris' waist. She slid down over him, then rolled her hips to massage him deeper inside. Her lips hung open, she peppered him in kisses while he throbbed to fill her. Chris' hands were strong, gentle, tight around her ebony hips. He pulsed up, sending ripples of pleasure through Sheba's body from thigh to breast. The heat between them swirled to an inferno of sensation. Their combined orgasm brought Sheba's groaning lips down on him, while every atom of Chris' being gyrated, overwhelmed.

Chris and Sheba reclothed just enough to deceive the nurses, if they ever decided to check in. It felt like hours that he lay there, awake with his fiancée's head on his chest. Sheba's shallow breath told him she was almost asleep.

Chris wanted more than anything to join her, but every time he shut his eyes, he saw the scales, talons, and eyes through Sheba, like they were right there in the room. Besides, he didn't want to miss a second of what time he had left. A tear ran from each eye while he counted the seconds until his first visitor came. It was no nurse, but the black form of a Squire. Its yellow face peeked through the curtain at him and Sheba.

"*She cannot follow*," he heard DA-Vos' voice in his mind, the first of countless side-effects from the Chrysum laced through his being. DA-Vos' face shimmered blue. Chris sucked down a shaking breath that stirred his lover. He would rather have relived the Shanghai mission a hundred times over.

"Sheba," Chris whimpered, "I have to go."

"Hm?" Sheba murmured. She stared up at him, longingly. Chris brushed his tears away, and forced a cold mask over his face.

"You..." he choked down the last of his hesitation. "You heard me."

"Go where, Chris? Dorothy said she was on her way," said Sheba, some awareness returning to her. "Besides, you're in no shape to..." her eyes wandered to the Squire in the door. Chris shrugged her head away, and sat up on the side of the bed. He hid the pain with his face turned for the wall.

"There was a change in plans. Dorothy just called, got me cleared." said Chris to the wall. He searched for anything to close in on, to use as a shield against her hands at his back. "You're a doctor of the mind, not the body. I'm in fine shape. It's *you* you should worry about, with your dream paranoia."

"What? Chris..." Sheba propped up.

"Before we can get married... you need to take care of you. I can't have you panicking every time you have a nightmare and calling me," said Chris. He bit his lip to keep himself from melting while he lost grip on himself. "Or trying to keep me from a mission." He stood and slipped his arms into his jacket.

"Ready to go, Major General?" said DA-Vos, in the doorway. Chris moved towards him, though he was Major General no longer. He wasn't human, or Dragon, or a machine either. He didn't know *what* he was, anymore.

"What... you're that Squire!" Sheba flung a finger at the robot. "Chris, what *is* this?"

"*Nothing, Sheba!*" Chris stomped back at her. For just a second, yellow light jumped through his eyes. His pupils sharpened to a black slit, then returned, fast enough to have been a trick. "You'd see that, if you weren't delusional." Numb as she was, Sheba moved for him, when he moved for the door.

"I don't believe this... I don't believe you!" she screamed.

"I don't want to be another way for you to run from your-self... I won't become part of your problem," Chris shook his head, "Maybe we can be what I thought we were, someday. When you're better. Good luck Sheba." He stepped out into the hallway. Chris cringed when he heard Sheba's steps behind him.

"*I'm sorry, Chris. You've got to do better,*" DA-Vos' voice rang through his mind. Chris sniffled down the tears about to burst through.

"I'm glad you came though. It was a tough mission, and I needed to get off," he said to her, "Maybe I'll swing by the apartment after the next one." That stopped Sheba dead in her tracks.

"You... you're not yourself," she whimpered.

"No, I'm not," said Chris. When he and DA-Vos left through the side door, past Tim's room, Sheba didn't follow.

"Ready to save the world?" said DA-Vos, under the night sky outside. In the cosmic darkness, Chris watched the radiance of the SkyLine. He wiped his eyes one last time before he gave up on stopping the flood.

"Consider yourself lucky if I can save *you* from *me*," growled Chris.

When he wanted nothing more than to turn back and find Sheba, he boarded the magnetrain. Chris felt the burden of the Skyline, of Mars, and all the lives caught between on his shoulders. All of it amounted to dust, compared to the weight of Sheba's words. *You're not yourself.*

She was still screaming into Chris' pillow, clinging to his scent, when a set of high heels clacked in the doorway. Sheba glanced up at a woman she'd met a handful of times, when she lived in the WCC barracks. The two never shared as much in common as they did the instant they connected eyes- shock.

"Where's Chris?" said Dorothy.

Over the next weeks into months, it was a question that became more and more difficult to answer.

In the watchless silver moonlight, with only a machine for company, Chris let himself go. He gave into the instinct stabbing at his new Chrysum-brain since he awoke, and transformed. Every border of his body loosened. His very atoms shook apart, creating a sort of Chris-shaped haze. Starting with his feet, that haze began to shift. When his particles realigned, it was not in the shape of feet, but scaly claws. His legs became two muscular trunks of armor. His fingers sharpened to silvery talons. His skull elongated. His teeth extended, sharpened. Chris' hair receded to shiny plates of scale. New bones burst from his back and swung open at a joint for the canvas of wings to grow. When Chris' form solidified, the only feature unchanged were the scars over his eyes- two yellow gemstones. He was Sheba's nightmare brought to life.

Even DA-Vos was paralyzed at the sight. He considered melting into the grass, to escape this beast. Then Chris held an arm out to him, expectant.

"You're not getting out of this now," Chris' dragonic voice hissed through DA-Vos' language processor. His face lit yellow, he saw what Chris wanted to do as clear as if it was his own idea. DA-Vos' body dissolved to coat Chris' scaly arm in a jet-black gauntlet.

His wings snapped open, filling the moon with the shape of a demon. Residents of the Lunar Station had no idea what was headed their way, nor did any in Chris' path to the Dragon's nest.

A WORD FROM THE AUTHOR

Hey there, I'm glad you enjoyed the first instalment of SkyLine, The Dragon Commander. I love to write Science Fiction and intertwine it with romance and mystical creatures.

For your enjoyment, I've included a preview of the next edition of SkyLine. The Captain, The Billionaire Boat and The Dragon Crusader. A lot has happened since the events of the first book, and I think you are going to be pleasantly surprised when you read all of it.

If you would like to get even awesome books from me and some of my recommendations from authors who write similar enticing novels, you can join my exclusive mailing list.

You'll get exclusive deals, special promotions and be the first

to partake in amazing stories and recommendations
from me.
See you on the space side. :)

https://kennedykingauthor.com/join-my-newsletter/

PREVIEW OF SKYLINE: THE CAPTAIN, THE BILLIONAIRE BOAT, AND THE DRAGON CRUSADER

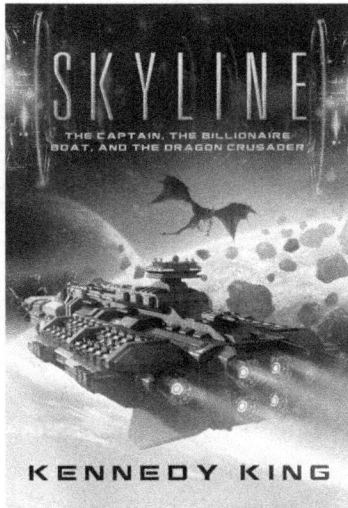

You can get SkyLine today from select book sellers,

https://kennedykingauthor.com/product/skyline-the-captain/

CHAPTER 1: OUTER RINGS

HE KNEW it wasn't really wind - there was no wind in space, even inside the SkyLine- but Drogan loved the rush of cosmic wind in his mane. He loved the graze of pressurized particles on the plate scales that covered his body. He loved the blaze of stars around him. Really, Drogan just loved being away from Mukurus. Away from his masters, both true and false. Besides, he could stretch his wings out here.

A canvas of jet black skin yawned between bony spokes that jutted from both shoulder blades. He unfurled them as wide as they would reach. Drogan's wings tilted. He glided from one edge of the SkyLine to the other. The talons of his toes sliced the inner barrier of pressurized atmosphere and energy. Blue wisps flickered up around Drogan from the break in the jetstream. He took his time while he was out this far, while there was no threat of being seen or heard. This part of the SkyLine was still under construction. No one but Drogan could be out here, this unfinished in-between. No human ship was capable. No Dragon had come so far. But then, he was neither of these. Like this part of the SkyLine, Drogan was in-between.

"We're coming up on the Neptune branch," a voice murmured across his mind. It had the inflection of a man, but the speaker was no human. Whether or not he was even *alive* had been the pastime subject of many a flight like this. Still, the understanding remained between Drogan and DA-Vos that they were all one another had. Beneath any frustration the two sometimes exchanged, they were bound to one fate. So, too, were they often bound in physical form. This was one such time; DA-Vos's nanomachine body formed into a solid black gauntlet around one of Drogan's arms.

"Maybe I should slow down," Drogan huffed, "It's not often we get the chance to just *fly*."

"Is that what you call this?" DA-Vos echoed through his mind.

"What would *you* call it?"

"Another mission. How many will it be, before we figure a way out of this? Another sixty years?" said DA-Vos.

"Careful, DA-Vos. Someone might think you have a mind of your own," Drogan prodded. His scaly lips curled in a fanged grin.

"I-I-I only mean... we're getting closer to the humans," stammered DA-Vos.

"You think I don't know that?" Drogan bit back. Quiet fell between them. Drogan took the opportunity to twirl into a corkscrew of wings. He spiraled all the way up to the top of the SkyLine. A focused flap of his wings sent him through the edge, out into the blackness of space. He flexed his wings, his dragonic limbs, and stopped still in the dark. Before him was the dusky vortex of stars called Antila 2. Somewhere in that beige stardust was the one who had a hold on them so tight, Drogan and DA-Vos could only speak freely here. Behind Drogan was his home galaxy. Until now, he hadn't been to the Milky Way in years.

"Does it *still* entertain you to torment me with existential dilemmas? After all this time?" DA-Vos asked.

"I'll stop as soon as *you* stop tormenting yourself," Drogan sighed. He flicked around to stare into the Milky Way. A far younger galaxy than Antila 2, its colors were twice as bright. Its stars were vibrant, full of fire and resources ripe for the taking. It was lucky for Drogan that his masters hadn't realized that yet, but they were getting an idea. Much as he hated to think about it, DA-Vos was right. Push *would* come to shove. When the breaking point came, the side Drogan fell on might not be the side he started from.

"Why do you think Machaeus can't hear us out here?" said DA-Vos.

"Why do you ask so many questions?" Drogan chuckled, though his lips didn't move. "Look who's stalling now." But then, he was in no rush himself. He fluttered backward through the darkness, eyes down on the SkyLine. A shimmering blue line through the black, it flowed like a river of energy. Human eyes couldn't see the nanomachines swarming around it, pressurizing and magnetizing the artificial atmosphere inside. "I'd guess it's because we're between. So far from both Antila 2 and the Milky Way. There's nothing to carry his thoughts."

"Then you think it *is* the fusion minerals that allow them to project their thoughts?" said DA-Vos.

"It makes sense. That's what you're made of, and we speak without our mouths. The only place we cannot reach Machaeus is in the blackness between Antila 2 and the Milky Way. There's no fusion minerals out here," Drogan figured. And that was it. Sixty years of reconnaissance and this was what Drogan and DA-Vos had to show for it.

Drogan spun and dove straight down into the SkyLine. A few pulses of his wings launched him to speeds surpassing most ships. With the added atmospheric acceleration inside the SkyLine, he would be inside the border of his home solar system in a day. By the time he passed the outerworld station on Neptune, Drogan and DA-Vos were a blur of color. From beyond the SkyLine, he tore by too fast for a bystander to tell he wasn't another small cruiser. Even those who caught a glimpse would never have guessed what the winged terror *really* was. Not in their wildest dreams.

"Watch it, Carl."

"Yeah," Carl huffed back. He had had about enough of being pushed around for one day. Jensen might be junior site manager, but Carl hadn't come all the way to the outer-worlds to oil crane arms. An hour of it was usually more than he could take. He'd been floating through the rings for triple that time now. He never thought the ripples through Saturn's gaseous surface or the ice caught in its orbits would cease to amaze him. He never pictured himself being bored, or frustrated. Not working the steel net of mines through the rings of Saturn. But then, Carl never pictured oiling crane collection arms for three hours. He had sweated through the clothes under his mining suit long ago. Now he was practically swimming.

"Carl!" Jensen's voice jumped through his earpiece.

"*What?*" Carl finally snapped.

"There a problem, son?" the junior site manager dug in.

"I've been out here long enough. The crane's oiled. I'm heading back in," Carl lowered to a simmer. He gripped the outside of the mining pod to throw himself back to the station hatch.

"Think you may have gotten our roles mixed, Carl. *I* tell *you* when the crane's oiled," rumbled Jensen, "If the crane arms don't work correctly, we can't mine the ice fields. If we can't mine the ice fields, we don't get the fusion minerals. If we don't get *those*, you can forget about your paycheck and go back to flipping burgers on the big blue mar-

"Jensen," Carl squeezed in.

"Now you're interrupting me, boy?" Jensen barked. He couldn't have known what Carl saw behind him. His mining cart faced the surface of the planet. Carl climbed up in front of its viewing window to point Jensen's eyes to the stations behind him.

"Look," he pointed. The mortal terror in Carl's eyes was enough to make him actually turn the wheel. Jensen's pod rotated around to find a tail of flame flick across one of the stations. It spread to one of the massive steel threads that comprised the net of mining stations.

"What in the hell..." Jensen muttered. Then he saw just what the hell it was: a flash of searing luminance jumped through a second station. It left a molten hole in its wake. Another plume of flame puffed from it, fed by the leak of oxygen within.

"Fly us back!" Carl shouted. He gripped the outside of the mining pod in a two-handed vice grip. Jensen's stunned eyes swallowed the fire. He could do nothing but watch. A figure about twice the size of a man zipped through the mining net. It halted a hundred feet from them with the snap of its massive wings. Carl and Jensen hardly had time to take it in - scales, yellow jewels for eyes, razor bladed hands and feet - before it raised its arm to them. A glossy black piece of armor on its hand morphed into a cannon barrel before them. A spark pulsed to life inside it. "Jensen!"

"A-a-alright!" Even Carl giving him orders was no match for the threat of that creature. Jensen jerked the helm of the pod to the side. The bolt of white that jumped from the creature's weapon missed them by inches. Carl felt the heat of it even through his suit. He heard the mighty flap of the beast's wings even in the emptiness of space. In a second, it perched atop the mining pod. The grasp of its talons crunched its outer sheathing.

"Storeroom?" a demonic voice snarled in the creature's throat, inches from Carl's face.

"Wha-wha-what?" Carl sputtered. He shrunk behind the frame of the mining pod.

"Storeroom?" it repeated. The claws of its hand etched five lines up the mining pod window.

"It wants to know where the damn storeroom is, Carl! Show it!" Jensen screamed. The beast's gemstone eyes flickered to the shouting site manager, and back to the suited miner. The glint of intelligence in its gaze haunted Carl for weeks to come. He lifted a shaky finger to a particular building in the mining net.

"O-o-over there. Station B-19," Carl told him. He flinched away from the slam of the beast's claw beside his head. Carl kept his pale face forward until the beast's fanged snout puffed fog across the side of his helmet. The slightest turn and it could tear his skull clean off.

"This guy bothering you?" asked the monstrous voice. Carl's head turned on a trembling axis. He took as good a look as he could get of the beast, without dying of sheer terror. He saw his own face in the mirror of its dark scales. The only things blacker than the beast was the space beyond Saturn and the gauntlet on its arm. "Is he?" The gravity of its voice demanded an answer. Carl gulped.

"Always," Carl whispered. The next he knew, he was hurtling through space, straight for the open hatch of a mining station. He hardly had time to feel the claw around the width of his chest. Carl didn't breathe until his boots touched down in the artificial gravity of the station. He felt around his suit for tears, for waterfalls of blood. Carl believed it even less than everything else he'd just seen, but he was unharmed. Whether or not Jensen would be able to say the same remained to be seen. He was busy screaming for his life while his mining pod hurtled through space, where the beast had thrown it. It cleared the outside of the mining net and kept going.

From the open station hatch, Carl had a perfect view of an event that would be etched in the annals of history, once the WCC tired of covering it up. The destruction of an eighth of Saturn's ring mines. The yellow-eyed fiend ripped from one station to the next, a dark streak against the light of the planet. Whatever crossed its path, it went straight through. Hunks of orbiting ice shattered against his dark armor. From within them, busts of Chrysum, the precious heart of all human fusion tech, stained the blackness of space silver. The creature kicked off from mining drones to keep path for B-19. They shot off into steel ropes of the mining net, breaking them apart. Fire and havoc followed in the wake of every raucous wing flap.

Sentry drones deployed from the security station. The yellow-eyed beast's gauntlet shifted back to a cannon. Blazing stripes of white jumped from its arm, straight through every machine. They floated away as useless, holey husks of steel. It was only so long before the human security team trotted out on the edge of the mining net, suited with resistance gear and armed with fusion rifles. Twenty of them took aim at the yellow-eyed demon through the icy storm. None of them got a shot off. The beast's cannon let out a sustained beam of pure white that swept along the mining net. The second its light retracted was the second flame exploded down the line it traced. Twenty men scorched in a second, two of them too horribly to mend. The beast's wings pulsed it straight towards B-19, and out of Carl's bewildered sight.

He never saw the beast again. He saw only more beams of blazing light from its cannon. He heard only the blast of combusting stations throughout the net. The beast vanished with the distant, sonic flap of wings and an entire month's stock of fusion mineral. Carl had no idea just then that he had survived an encounter with the outlaw of the outerworlds, Drogan himself.

CHAPTER 4: BEFORE DAWN

"HOWARD," Marcus rumbled on their way from the office. Dawn and Miller stopped along with him, until the Councilman specified, "Another word or two. In private." Dawn hung back a second longer with the shared wonder of what could be inappropriate for their *whole* task force to know. But Marcus was a patient man, and Miller had done this dance before. He gave Dawn a gentle nudge towards the door. The two left Howard alone in the room at the speed of drying paint.

"What can I help you with, Councilman?" asked Howard when the office door sealed him inside.

"You mean *besides* running IT for an autonomous ship and bringing back the first interplanetary outlaw?" Marcus laughed. When the extent of Howard's rise expressed itself as a lip twitch, Marcus reverted to business mode. "I need you to collect and review research from a few labs when you get to Neptune." Howard crossed his arms. It took the grate of every tooth in his mouth to muster this much confrontational energy.

"Research? I'm sorry... I'm afraid I work for Wellsworth," said Howard.

"You're too smart to play dumb, Howard. Your father worked for Wellworth. Your grandfather worked for Wellsworth. The company office is on Mars, yet their paychecks- along with yours- come from central Shanghai," said Marcus. *Straight from the horse's mouth,* Howard thought. Wellsworth, the WCC - two names for one monster.

"There are labs out as far as Neptune?" said Howard after a tense gulp.

"There are."

"I... didn't think the outerworlds had much of anything on them yet. The SkyLine to Neptune was only finished two years ago," said Howard.

"Yes, it was. And there *isn't* much out there. Not according to documentation," said Marcus, "You don't have to dance around what you want to say, Howard. It's one of the few perks that comes with the weight of that giant brain in your head. It would be very hard to replace you." He extended a hand of invitation as if he were really there in the room. As it stood, Howard felt more in the chill of a phantom than the presence of any man.

"The only reason you would build a lab out so far is... to avoid WCC sanctions," Howard theorized.

"Wellsworth *is* an independent health practice, regardless of where the money to pay for it comes from," said Marcus, "What they do out so far, I'm afraid, is out of our hands until we establish a Consulate there."

"Like you did on Mars," smoldered Howard. The stories handed down from his grandfather, Tim, scorched fresh across his brain. He imagined the stony crimson hallways of underground lab offices and treatment rooms more vividly than ever. The spread of nanomachine-maintained terradomes across Mars had brought with it an explosion of farming and mining colonies. With the growth in jobs and population came the call for the first off-world WCC consulate. Just like that, the scales had tipped in favor of galactic expansion. Suddenly, there was a place for people to *go*, and they did. Howard's grandfather did. His father's decision to return their family to the fading rock called Earth was still a touchy subject with his mother, especially since the passing of the box twenty years ago.

"Exactly," said Marcus, "A new, unmonitored planet is the only place certain types of progress can happen, Howard."

"I... could report this," Howard dared. A pearl of sweat rolled down his chest under his shirt.

"You could," Marcus chuckled, "I'm afraid you'd have to go up the totem pole a ways to find someone who could do something about it. You'd need someone who *didn't* hand this order down to me, on its way to you. That particular someone might be hard to find." Howard's nails scraped across either side of his seat, beside his legs.

"Relax, Howard. It doesn't need to come to that. I only need you to trust me a little ways and you'll see. We're getting close. Like your grandfather, we believe the perpetrators of these mineral thefts and the attack on Precinct 117 are the same. The entity called, in some unsavory circles... Dragons."

"Many people with institutionalized family members would call you cruel for saying something like that," Howard lashed back. Marcus leaned back, eyes wide at the unprecedented rage - but then it wasn't so much Howard's, as the channeled anger of another.

"Which is why I chose only to tell *you* this. I trust your judgment more than most anyone else's on this. Reports from Wellsworth Labs on Neptune tell us that they've had a few breakthroughs with their 3D patients. Spikes in their conditions coincide with the mineral thefts. If we can use this information to find the culprits, and it *does* turn out to be related..." Marcus trailed off intentionally. One of his favorite coercion techniques was to let people come to their "own" conclusion just this way. They were always more apt to pursue it.

"We might find a way to undo the effects of 3D," Howard played along. As someone who rarely trusted a conclusion he didn't arrive at himself, he wasn't *so* easily coerced.

"We might. If you can find something in the research," Marcus nodded. There was the pitch. It was up to Howard to catch it or let it go. The nagging voice of grandpa Tim in the back of his mind was what gave him the courage. *Finish what I started, with Sheba.*

"I will," said Howard. "I assume you don't want the others knowing about the labs?"

"If there's one thing to get straight about this whole operation, it's the less Miller's crew knows, the better," Marcus affirmed.

"And Dawn?" The curve of Marcus' smirk had just a hint too much irony for Howard's liking.

"If she needs to fly, she'll need to know everything you know. Otherwise... stay quiet about it. I think you'll find it in your best interest to keep her safe," said Marcus.

"It's in my best interest to keep *everyone* safe," said Howard, "However little I can do."

"Oh, have a little faith in yourself," Marcus waved him off, "Or take some of mine with you, on your way out. You can go now." On his way to the door, Howard shot one last look back at the man on the screen.

"Understood. See you on Neptune."

"If you *see* me, Mr. Carver, something will have gone very wrong." With that, and an unsettled pit in the bottom of his gut, Howard left the office of Councilman Marcus Brass. He was halfway through the door when he bumped shoulders with a metal demon. Howard jumped back, astonished to find it was actually a woman, in part anyway.

"So-so-sorry," Howard sputtered. The part of her mouth that was still human lips smirked. The steel plates in the left corner of them could only open slightly. That metal continued up the entire left side of her face, all the way to her graying hairline. A black orb with a yellow lens spun around in a steel crater substitute for an eye socket. Her human eye was a dim, slate blue. The contrast was downright ghastly.

"For what? Existing, in my way? You get a pass this time," rasped the old woman. A steel plate arm, held by joints of bolts and brackets, creaked up to grasp Howard's shoulder.

"Tha-thank you?" he managed, just before the woman shoved past him. Her mechanical legs popped and pumped her into Marcus' office. Aside from part of her face and long twists of gray hair, the only human part of her was her right arm. An intricate illustration of dragons in flight twisted around it, inscribed in ink. The sliding door shut her inside the office with Marcus. The hairs on the back of Howard's neck didn't lay flat for another hour.

"Morgan," Marcus greeted half of a woman he used to know. The other half of the thing before him was engineered in a lab not far from the Consulate.

"Marcus," Morgan answered. Her yellow eye flickered alight when she blinked. "Been a while since you called."

"Well this isn't a mission I can afford to trust to humans alone," Marcus smirked, "I just finished briefing the primary task force, so forgive me if I'm brief. You're familiar with the SS Arcadia?"

"Everyone in my line of work is," said Morgan.

"I need you to trail it, wherever it goes. If the task force on board fails in their assignment, *you* are to complete it. Otherwise, keep a distance and observe," Marcus told her. Morgan's remaining eyebrow propped up.

"And what assignment would that be?"

"Bringing back someone... I think he might be an old friend of yours," said Marcus.

"How old?"

"You haven't seen him in sixty years if I'm right. Not since the incident at Precinct 117. Do you recall?" Marcus dug, just to see what he would find in Morgan. Not the gold of fury as he expected, but the dark spite of oil.

"Of course I do. Better half of me was ripped away there. The other half was born shortly after, on a conveyor belt," said Morgan, "Are you telling me you think you know where Christopher Droan is?" Marcus only grinned. Blood flooded the dried out caverns of Morgan's desiccating heart. Even if it came to fists, the idea of seeing her old Major General again made her more alive than she'd been in years. "So... where am I going?"

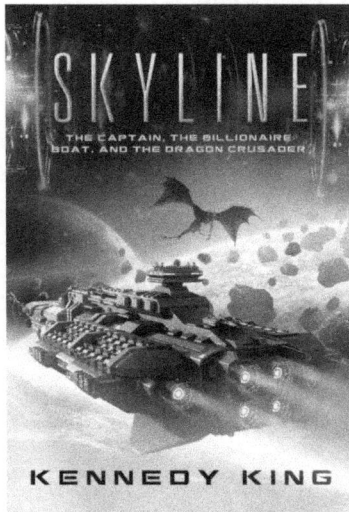

You can get SkyLine today from select book sellers, https://kennedykingauthor.com/product/skyline-the-captain/

ALSO BY KENNEDY KING

Love of Olympia : Tournament of Stars (The Olympia Gold Series Book 1)

https://kennedykingauthor.com/product/love-of-olympia/

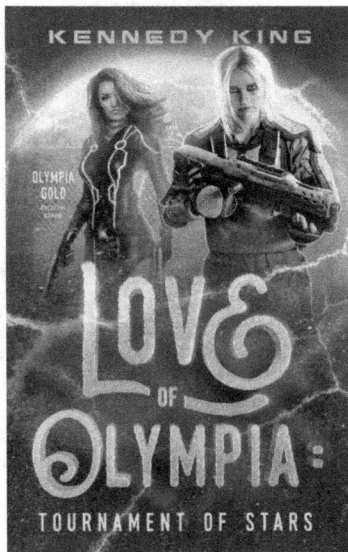

Live in chains, or die trying to become a free woman?

Those were the choices of the Olympia Gold.

The competition I'm participating in right now.

One contestant in the other team caught my interest. *Galia. No man has ever made me feel the way she has.*

But she's such a reckless, gorgeous, pompous woman! Even so, perhaps she can help us...

The only thing standing between us and freedom are six gruelling, fatal challenges and even more bloodthirsty crews battling for the glory of Olympia.

I'm destined to work under the boot of the Corporation for the rest of my life, to pay the debt of my dead father's addiction to the most violent competition in the galaxy.

Everyone in my crew are servants. My best friend Devin and I obeyed the Totalitarian Corporation all of our lives.

The other teams have more training, credits and are armed to the teeth with the most advanced tech the black markets have.

If we fail, the Corporation will destroy us; take our lives and everything we ever cared for.

Our odds are low, but I never felt so strongly about anything else.

Is my will to survive enough to see us through?

EXPERIENCES BY OTHER AUTHORS IN THE MIND OF KHAN STUDIOS UNIVERSE

Entropy's Allegiance by Mikkell K Khan

https://mikkellkhan.com/product/entropys-allegiance-magic-of-the-old-arts-book-1/

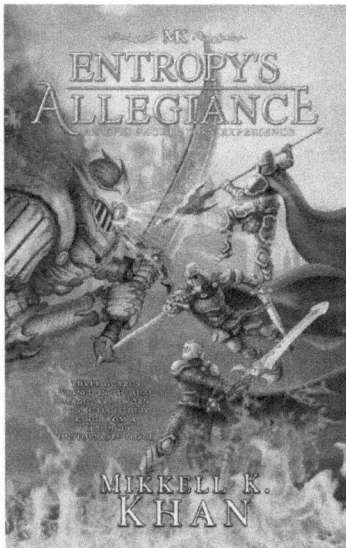

After all the newly appointed king's defenses have fallen, it's up to his three loyal guards versed in the magic of the old arts to prevent a seemingly unstoppable force from assassinating him.

THE ENIXAR: THE SORCERER'S CONQUEST
BY MIKKELL K KHAN

https://mikkellkhan.com/product/the-enixar-the-sorcerers-conquest-the-enixar-book-1/

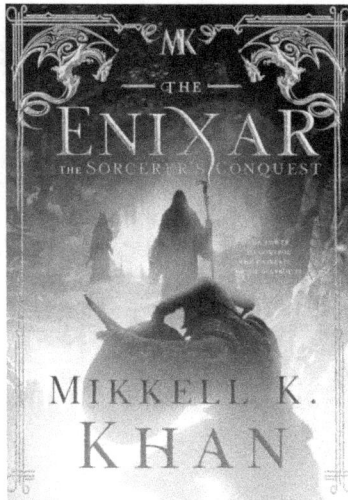

A sorcerer king, his wise advisor, and a young sorceress hiding her growing powers race to find an ancient power once thought lost.

The power to control the universe... or to destroy it.

The Enixar : The Sorcerer's Conquest is a novella and dynamic introduction to an epic fantasy series you won't be able to put down! Complete with a strong female protagonist, Sorcerer King, and political intrigue, this series dives into the core of Epic Fantasy and Science Fiction that fans will love.

AUDIO EXPERIENCES FROM THE MIND OF KHAN STUDIOS UNIVERSE

If you would love to immerse yourself in the Mind of Khan Studios stories even more, we offer an incredible audiobook library of most of our selections with many retailers.

To get your copy of this novel as an audio book today, and for a consistently updated list of new and upcoming audio experiences, you can join our mailing list here, https://mindofkhan.com/mailing-list/ or check out our library of currently released titles here,

https://audio.mindofkhan.com/.

CPSIA information can be obtained
at www.ICGtesting.com
Printed in the USA
LVHW051301241021
701370LV00014B/1652